Wilhelmine Heimburg

Gertrude's Marriage

Wilhelmine Heimburg

Gertrude's Marriage

ISBN/EAN: 9783337319359

Printed in Europe, USA, Canada, Australia, Japan

Cover: Foto ©Andreas Hilbeck / pixelio.de

More available books at **www.hansebooks.com**

"THERE WAS A CRASH AND A SPLITTING OF WOOD AND THE DOOR
WAS BURST OPEN."

Page 202.

GERTRUDE'S MARRIAGE

W. HEIMBURG

TRANSLATED FROM THE GERMAN

By MRS. J. W. DAVIS

ILLUSTRATED

NEW YORK

WORTHINGTON CO., 747 BROADWAY

1889

GERTRUDE'S MARRIAGE.

CHAPTER I.

"REALLY, Frank, if I were in your place I shouldn't know whether to laugh or cry. It has always been the height of my ambition to have a fortune left me, but as with everything in this earthly existence, I should have my preferences.

"Upon my word, Frank, I am sorry for you. Here you are with an inheritance fallen into your lap that you never even dreamed of, a sort of an estate, a few hundred acres and meadows, a little woodland, a garden run wild, a neglected dwelling-house, and for stock four spavined Andalusians, six dried-up old cows, and above all an old aunt who apparently unites the attributes of both horses and cows in her own person. Boy, at least wring your

1

hands or scold or do something of the sort, but don't stand there the very picture of mute despair ! "

Judge Weishaupt spoke thus in comic wrath to his friend Assessor Linden, who sat opposite him. Before them on the table stood a bottle of Rhine wine with glasses, and the eyes of the person thus addressed rested on the empty bottle with a thoughtful expression, as if he could read an answer on the label.

It was a large room in which they were sitting, a sort of garden-hall, furnished very simply and in an old-fashioned style, with two birchen corner-cupboards, which in our grandmother's time served the purpose of the present elegant buffets, and which, instead of costly majolica, displayed painted and gold-rimmed cups behind their glass doors; with a large sofa, whose black horse-hair covering never for a moment suggested the possibility of soft luxurious repose ; with six simply-constructed cane-seated chairs grouped about the large table, and finally, with several dubious family portraits, among which especially to be noted was the pastel portrait of a youthful fair-haired beauty, whose impossibly small mouth wore an embarrassed smile as if to say: "I beg you to believe that I did not really look so silly as this!" And over all this bright orange-colored curtains shed a peculiarly unpleasant light.

The door of the room was open and as if in compensation for all this want of taste, a wonderful prospect spread itself out before the eye. Lofty wooded mountain tops, covered with rich foliage which the autumn frosts had already turned into brilliant colors, formed the background; close by, the neglected garden, picturesque enough in its wild state, and shimmering through the trees, the red pointed roofs of the village; the whole veiled with the soft haze of an October morning, which the rays of the sun had not yet dispersed. The regular strokes of the flails on the threshing floors of the estate had a pleasant sound in the clear morning air.

The young man's dark eyes strayed away from the wine-bottle; he started up suddenly and went to the door.

"And in spite of all that, Richard, it is a charming spot," he said warmly. "I have

always had a great liking for North Germany.
I assure you 'Faust' is twice as interesting
here, where the Brocken looks down upon
you. Don't croak so like an old raven any
more, I beg of you. I shall never forget
Frankfort, but neither shall I miss it too
much—I hope."

"Heaven forbid!" cried the little man, still
playing with the empty wine-glass. "You
don't pretend to say—"

But Linden interrupted him. "I don't pretend anything, but I am going to try to be a
good farmer, and I am going to do this, Richard, not only because I must, but because I
really like this queer old nest; so say no more,
old fellow."

"Well, good luck to you!" replied the
other, coming up to his friend and looking
almost tenderly into the handsome, manly
face.

"I have really nothing to say against this
playing at farming if I only know how and
where.—You see, Frank, if I were not such a
poverty-stricken wretch, I would say to you
this minute : ' Here, my boy, is a capital of so
much ; now go to work and get the moth-

eaten old place into some kind of order.'
Things cannot go on as they are. But—
well, you know—" he ended, with a sigh.

Frank Linden made no reply, but he whistled softly a lively air, as he always did when
he wished to drive away unpleasant thoughts.

"O yes, whistle away," muttered the little
man, "it is the only music you are likely to
hear, unless it is the creaking of a rusty hinge
or the concert of a highly respectable family
of mice which have settled in your room—
brr—Frank! Just imagine this lonely hole in
winter—snow on the mountains, snow on the
roads, snow in the garden and white flakes in
the air! Good Heavens! What will you do
all the long evenings which we used to spend
in the Taunus, in the Bockenheimer Strasse, or
in the theatre? Who will play euchre with
you here? For whom will you make your
much-admired poems? I am sure they won't
be understood in the village inn. Ah, when I
look at you and think of you moping here
alone, and with all your cares heavy upon
you!"

He sighed.

"I will tell you something, Frank, joking

aside," he continued. "You must marry.
And I advise you in this matter not to lay so
much stress on your ideal ; pass over for once
the sylph-like forms, liquid eyes and sweet
faces in favor of another advantage which
nothing will supply the place of, in our
prosaic age. Don't bring me a poor girl,
Frank, though she were a very pearl of women.
In your position it would be perfect folly, a
sin against yourself and all who come after
you. It won't make the least difference if
your fine verses don't exactly fit her. You
wouldn't always be making poetry, even to
the loveliest woman. O yes, laugh away !"

He brushed the ashes from his cigar. " In
Frankfort—if you had only chosen—you
might have done something. But you were
quite dazzled by that little Thea's lovely eyes.
How often I have raged about it ! When a
man has passed his twenty-fifth year he
really ought to be more sensible."

Frank Linden was obstinately silent, and
the little man knew at once that he had as he
used to say, "put his foot in it."

"Come, Frank, don't be cross," he con-

"BOTH GENTLEMEN TURNED TOWARD THE SPEAKER."

Page 7.

tinued, "perhaps there are rich girls to be had here too."

"O to be sure, sir, to be sure," sounded behind him, "rich girls and pretty girls; our old city has always been celebrated for them."

Both gentlemen turned toward the speaker; the judge only to turn away at once with an angry shrug, Frank Linden to greet him politely.

"I have brought the papers you wanted," continued the new-comer, a little man over fifty with an incredibly small pointed face over which a sweet smile played, a sanctimonious man in every motion and gesture.

"I am much obliged, Mr. Wolff," said Frank Linden, taking the papers.

"If there is anything else I can do for you —Miss Rosalie will testify that I was always ready to help your late uncle."

"I am a perfect stranger here," replied the young squire, "it may be that I shall require your help."

"I shall feel highly honored, Mr. Linden— Yes, and as I said before, if you should want to make acquaintances in the city there are the Tubmans, the Schenks, the Meiers and

the Hellbours and above all the Baumhagens
—all rich and pleasant families, Mr. Linden.
You will be received with open arms, there's
always a dearth of young men in our little
city. The gentlemen of the cavalry—you
know, I suppose—only want to amuse themselves—shall be only too glad in case you—"

The judge interrupted him with a loud
clearing of his throat.

"Frank," he said, dryly, "what tower is
that up there on the hill? You were studying
the map yesterday!"

"St. Hubert's Tower," replied the young
man, going towards him.

"Belongs to the Baron von Lobersberg,"
interposed Wolff.

"That doesn't interest me in the least,"
muttered the judge, gazing at the tower
through his closed hand for want of a glass.

"I have the honor to bid you good-morn-
ing," said Wolff, "must go over to Lobersberg."

The judge nodded curtly; Linden accompanied the agent to the door and then came
slowly back.

"Now please explain to me," burst out his

friend, "where you picked up that fellow—
that rat, I should say, who pushes himself into
your society so impudently."

Frank Linden's dark eyes turned in aston-
ishment to the angry countenance of the
judge.

"Why, Richard, he was my uncle's right-
hand man, his factotum, and lastly, he has
something to say about my affairs, for unhap-
pily, he holds a large mortgage on Niendorf."

"That does not justify him in the imperti-
nent manner which he displays towards you,"
replied his friend.

"O my dear little Judge," said the young
man in excuse, "he looks on me as a new-
comer, an ignoramus in the sacred profession
of farming. You—"

"And I consider him a shady character!
And some day, my dear boy, you will say to
me, 'Richard, God knows you were right
about that man—the fellow is a rascal.'"

"Do you know," cried Frank Linden, between jest and earnest, "I wish I had left you
quietly in your lodging in the Goethe-Platz.
You will spoil everything here for me with
your gloomy views. Come, we will take a

turn through the garden; then, unfortunately, it will be time for you to go to the station, if you wish to catch the Express."

He took the arm of his grumbling friend and drew him with him along the winding path, on which already the withered leaves were lying.

"I am sure the fellow has a matrimonial agency somewhere," muttered the judge, grimly.

As they turned the corner of the neglected shrubbery, they saw an old woman slowly pacing up and down the edge of the little pond.

"For Heaven's sake!" began the little man again, "just look at that figure, that cap with the monstrous black bow, that astonishing dress with the waist up under the arms, and what a picturesque fashion of wearing a black shawl—and, goodness! she has got a red umbrella. My son, she probably uses it to ride out on the first of May—brr—and that is your only companion!"

It was indeed a remarkable figure, the old woman wandering up and down with as much dignity as if one of the faded pastel pictures in the garden hall had suddenly come to life.

"Shall I call her?" asked Frank Linden, smiling.

"Heaven forbid!" cried the other. "This neighborhood of the Blocksberg is really uncanny—your Mr. Wolff looks like Mephistopheles in person, and this—well, I won't say what—she is really a serious charge for you, Frank."

The wonderful figure had long since disappeared behind the bushes, when the young man answered, abstractedly,

"You see things in too gloomy a light, Richard. How can this poor, feeble old woman, almost on the verge of the grave, possibly be a burden to me? She lives entirely shut up in her own room."

"But I will venture to say that she will be forever wanting something of you. When she is cold the stove will be in fault, when she has rheumatism you will have to shoot a cat for her. She will meddle in your affairs, she will mislay your things, and will vex you in a thousand ways. Old aunts are only invented to torment their fellow-men. But no matter, make your own beer and drink it all down. But I think it must be time to go, the Express won't wait."

Linden looked at his watch, nodded, and went hastily to the house to order the carriage.

His friend followed him thoughtfully; at length he muttered a suppressed, "Confound it! Such a splendid young fellow to sit and suck his paws in this hole of a peasant village! What sort of a figure will he cut among the rich proprietors of this blessed country? I wish his old uncle had chosen anybody on earth for his heir, only not *him*—much as he pretends to like it. What a career he might have made! And now he will just bury himself in this hole—confound Niendorf! If I only had him at home in gay Frankfort—O— it is—"

A quarter of an hour later the friends were rolling towards the city in a rather old-fashioned carriage. Behind them was the quiet little Harz village, and before them rose the many-towered city.

They had not far to go; they reached their destination in an hour's time, and the carriage stopped before the stately railroad station. Silently as they had come they got the ticket and had the baggage weighed, and Linden did not speak till they reached the platform.

"Greet Frankfort for me, Richard, and all my friends. Write to me when you have time. See that I get my furniture and books soon, and many thanks for your company so far."

The judge made a deprecating gesture. "I wish to Heaven I could take you back with me, Frank," he said, in a softer tone. "You don't know how I shall miss you. You know what a bad correspondent I am, you are much better at writing than I, and you will have more time for it, too—"

The whistle and the rumbling of the approaching train cut him short; in another moment he was in a *coupé*.

"Good-bye, Frank—come nearer for a moment, old fellow—remember if you are ever in any serious difficulty, write to me at once. If I should not be able to help you myself—you know my sister is in good circumstances—"

One more hand-shake, one more look into a pair of true, manly eyes, and Frank Linden stood alone on the platform. He turned slowly away, and walked towards his carriage. He had his foot on the step when he be-thought himself, and ordered the coachman to drive to the hotel, for he had something to do in town.

He was so entirely under the influence of the uncomfortable feeling which parting from a friend creates, that he took the road into town in no very cheerful mood. On entering the city he turned aside and followed a de-serted path which led along the well-pre-served old city wall. He did not in the least know where he was going; he had nothing to do here, he knew no one, but he must look about a little in the neighboring town. It seemed, in fact, well entitled to its repu-tation as an old German imperial city; the castle, with the celebrated cathedral, towered up defiantly on the steep crags; several slender church towers rose from out the multitude of red pointed roofs, and the old wall, broken at regular intervals by clumsy square watch-towers, surrounded the old town like a firm chain.

He took delight in the beautiful picture,

and as he walked on his fancy painted the magnificent imperial city waking out of its slumber of a thousand years. After awhile he stopped and looked up to one of the gray towers.

"Really it is almost like the Eschenheim Gate in Frankfort," he said half aloud; "what wonderful springs the thoughts make!"

Suddenly he found himself back in the present; scarcely four weeks ago he had passed through that beautiful gate, without dreaming that he would so soon see its companion in North Germany. Like lightning out of blue sky this inheritance which made him posessor of Niendorf had come upon him. How it had happened to occur to his grandfather's old brother to select *him* out of the multitude of his relatives for his heir still remained an unsolved problem, and he could only refer it to the especial liking for his mother whom the eccentric old man had always shown a preference for.

He had felt when he received the news as if a golden shower had fallen into his lap; it is difficult living in a city of millionaires on the salary of an assessor. And then—he

had received a wound there in that brilliant
bewildering life, and the scar still made itself
felt at times—for instance when an elegant
equipage dashed by him—black horses with
liveries of black and silver and on the light-gray
cushions a woman's figure, dark ostrich feathers
waving above a face of marble whiteness, the
luxuriant gold brown hair fastened in a knot
on the neck and ah! looking so coldly at him
out of her great blue eyes. After such a
meeting he felt depressed for days. "A
milliner's doll, a heartless woman," he called
her bitterly, but he had once believed quite
the reverse a whole year long till one morning
he saw her betrothal in the paper. She married a banker who had often served as the
butt of her ridicule. But—he had a mil-
lion!

Ah, how gladly had he gone out of her
neighborhood, how rejoiced he had been
to turn his back on the great world, with
what happiness he had written to his mother
and what had he found!

But no matter! The steward whom he had
for the present seemed a capable fellow; he
would not spare himself in any respect and

then—Wolff. He could not understand what had set Weishaupt so against the man.

He had now been wandering for some time through the busiest streets of the town. He asked for the hotel where his coachman was to wait for him. He now entered the market-place in the midst of which the statue of Roland stands. A stately Rathhaus in the style of the Renaissance stood on the western side of the square, and lofty elegant patrician houses with pointed gables surrounded it ; some adorned with bow-windows, some with the upper stories overhanging till it seemed as if they must lose their balance. Only two or three buildings were of later date, and even in these care had been taken to preserve the mediæval character.

Agreeably surprised, Linden stopped and his glance passed critically over the front of the lofty building before which he had chanced to pause. Three tall stories towered one above another; over the great arched door-way rose a dainty bow-window which extended through all the stories and stretched up into the blue October sky as a stately tower, fin-ished at the top with a weather-vane. The

2

window in the *bel-etage* was divided into small
diamond panes—that was an "æsthetic" dwelling, no doubt. In the second story rich
lace curtains shimmered behind large clear
panes, and a very garden of fuchsias and
pinks waved and nodded from the plants
outside. If a lovely girl's face would only
appear above them now, the picture would be
complete.

But nothing of the kind was to be seen,
and casting one more glance at the artistic
ironwork of the staircase, the attentive spec-
tator turned and crossed the market-place
to the hotel in order to dine. As it was
already late he was the only guest in the
spacious dining-room. He ate his dinner
with all speed, and began his wanderings
through the streets again.

Behind the Rathhaus he plunged into a labyrinth of narrow streets and alleys, then passing through an archway he entered unexpectedly a square surrounded by tall linden trees
half stripped of their leaves, which, grave and
solemn, seemed to be watching over a large
church. It seemed as though everybody was
dead in this place; only a few children were

playing among the dry leaves, and an old woman limped into a sunny corner, otherwise the deepest silence reigned.

A side door of the church stood open ; he crossed over and entered into the silent twilight of the sacred place ; he took off his hat, and, surprised by the noble simplicity of the building, he gazed at the slender but lofty columns and the rich vaulting of the choir. Then he walked down the middle aisle between the artistically carved stalls, brown with age. He delighted in them, for he had the greatest admiration for the beautiful forms of the Renaissance, and he was doubly pleased, for he had not expected to find anything of the kind here.

Here he suddenly stopped ; there at the font, above which the white dove soared with outspread wings, he saw three women. Two of them seemed to be of the lower class ; the elder, probably the midwife, held the child, tossing it continually ; the other, in a plain black woollen dress and shawl, a young matron, looked at the child with eyes red with weeping ; a third had bent down towards her ; the sexton, who was pouring the water

into the basin, concealed her completely for
the moment and Linden saw only the train of
a dark silk dress on the stone floor.

And now a soft flexible woman's voice
sounded in his ear: " Don't cry so, my good
Johanna, you will have a great deal of comfort yet with the little thing—don't cry !

" Engleman, you had better call the clergyman—my sister does not seem to come, she
must have been detained ; we will not wait
any longer."

The speaker turned towards the mother, and
Frank Linden looked full into the face of the
young girl. It was not exactly beautiful, this
fine oval, shaded by rich golden brown hair ;
the complexion was too pale, the expression
too sad, the corners of the mouth too much
drawn down, but under the finely pencilled
brows a pair of deep blue eyes looked out at
him, clear as those of a child, wistful and ap-
pealing, as if imploring peace for the sacred
rite.

It might often happen that strangers
entered the beautiful church and made a dis-
turbance—at least so Frank Linden inter-
preted the look. Scarcely breathing, he

leaned against one of the old stalls, and his
eyes followed every movement of the slender,
girlish figure, as she took the child in her arms
and approached the clergyman.

"Herr Pastor," sounded the soft voice,
"you must be content with *one* sponsor, for
unfortunately my sister has not come."

The clergyman raised his head. "Then
you might, Mrs. Smith—" he signed to the
elder woman.

Frank Linden stood suddenly before the
font beside the young girl; he hardly knew
himself how he got there so quickly.

"Allow me to be the second sponsor," he
said.—"I came into the church by chance, a
perfect stranger here; I should be sorry to miss
the first opportunity to perform a Christian
duty in my new home."

He had obeyed a sudden impulse and he
was understood. The gray-haired clergyman
nodded, smiling. "It is a poor child, early
left fatherless, sir," he replied. "The father
was killed four weeks before its birth—you
will be doing a good work—are you satisfied?" he said, turning to the mother. "Well

then—Engelman, write down the name of the godfather in the register."

"Carl Max Francis Linden," said the young man.

And then they stood together before the pastor, these two who a quarter of an hour ago had had no knowledge of one another; she held the sleeping child in her arms; she had not looked up, the quick flush of surprise still lingered on the delicate face, and the simple lace on the infant's cushion trembled slightly.

The clergyman spoke only a few words, but they sank deep into the hearts of both. Linden looked down on the brown drooping head beside him, the two hands rested on the infant's garments, two warm young hands close together, and from the lips of both came a clear distinct " Yes " in answer to the clergyman's questions. When the rite was ended, the young girl took the child to its weeping mother and pressed a kiss on the small red cheek, then she came up to Linden and her eyes gazed at him with a mixture of wonder and gratitude.

"I thank you, sir," she said, laying her

small hand in his for a moment. "I thank you in the name of the poor woman—it was so good of you."

Then with a proud bend of her small head she went away, the heavy silk of her dress making a slight rustling about her as she walked. She paused a moment at the door in the full daylight and looked back at him as he stood motionless by the font looking after her; it seemed as if she bent her head once more in greeting and then she disappeared.

Frank Linden remained behind alone in the quiet church. Who could she be who had just stood beside him? A slight jingling caused him to turn round; the sexton was coming out of the sacristy with his great bunch of keys.

"You want to shut up the church, my friend?" he said. "I am going now." Then as if he had thought of something he came back a few steps. "Who was the young lady?" was on his lips to ask, but he could not bring it out, he only gazed at the glowing colors in the painted glass of the lofty window.

"They are very fine," said the sexton,

"and are always much admired; that one is dated 1511, the Exodus of the children of Israel, a gift from the Abbess Anna from the castle up there. They say she had a great liking for this church, and it is the finest church far and wide too, our St. Benedict's."

Frank Linden nodded.

"You may be right," he said, abstractedly. Then he gave the man a small sum for the baby and went away.

Soon after, his carriage was rolling away towards home. The outlines of the mountains rose dark against the red evening sky, and the church-tower of Niendorf came nearer and nearer.

Nothing seemed strange to him now as it had been this morning; the first slight happy feeling of home-coming was growing in his heart. On the top of the hill he turned again and looked back at the city, where the castle looked to him like an old acquaintance, and hark! The faint sound of a bell was wafted towards him on the evening breeze; perhaps from St. Benedict's tower?

CHAPTER II.

GERTRUDE BAUMHAGEN had quickly crossed the quiet square, had opened a door in the opposite wall, and was at home. She passed rapidly through the box-edged path of the old-fashioned garden, and across a quiet spacious court into the house. In the large vaulted hall, she found her brother-in-law standing beside a tall velocipede. He was dressed elegantly and according to the latest fashion, a costly diamond sparkled on the blue cravat, while he wore another on his white hand. He was fair-haired, with pink cheeks, and a small moustache on his upper lip, and was perhaps about thirty. A servant was occupied in cleaning the shining steel of the bicycle with a piece of chamois leather.

" Are you going for a ride, Arthur ? " asked the young girl, pleasantly.

" I am going to make off, Gertrude," he replied, peevishly. " What on earth can I do

25

at home? Jenny has got a ladies' tea party
again to-day by way of variety—and what am·
I to do? I am going with Carl Röben to
Bodenstadt—a man must look out for himself
a little."

"I am just going up to your house," said
the young girl. " I am cross with Jenny and
am going to scold her."

"You will be lucky then if you don't come
off second best, my dear sister-in-law," cried
Arthur Fredericks, laughing.

She shook her head gravely, and mounted
the broad staircase, whose dark carved balustrade harmonized well with the crimson
Smyrna carpet which covered the steps, held
down by shining brass rods. Huge laurel-
trees in tubs stood on either side of the tall
door, which led to the first floor. On the left,
the staircase went on to the upper story.
Gertrude Baumhagen pressed on the button
of the electric bell and instantly the door was
opened by a servant-maid in a brilliantly
white apron, while a clear voice called out,

"Yes, yes, I am at home—you have come
just in time, Gertrude."

In the large entrance hall, which was finished in old German style, a young matron stood before a magnificent buffet, busied in taking out all manner of silver-plate from the open cupboard. She wore a dainty little lace cap on her light brown hair, and a house-dress of fine light blue cashmere, richly trimmed with lace. She was very pretty, even now when she was pouting, but there was no resemblance between the two sisters.

"You are not even dressed yet, Jenny?" cried the young girl. "Then I might have waited a good while in the church. It was really very awkward, your not coming."

The young matron stopped and set down the great glass dish encircled by two massive silver snakes, in dismay. Then she clapped her hands and began to laugh heartily.

"There now!" she cried, "this whole day I have been going about the house with a feeling that there was something I had to do, and I couldn't think what it was. O that is too rich! Caroline, you might have reminded me!" she continued, turning to the maid, who was just laying a heavy linen table-cloth on the massive oak-table in the middle of the room.

"Mrs. Fredericks laid down to sleep and said expressly that I was not to wake her before four o'clock," said the maid in her own defence.

"Well, so I did," yawned the young matron; "I was so tired, his lordship was in a bad temper, and the baby was so frightfully noisy. It is no great misfortune, either; I can easily make up for it by sending her something to-morrow."

"Why, Jenny! Have you forgotten that it was I who told Johanna that you and I would be godmothers? I thought it was our *duty*—the man was killed in our factory."

"O fiddle-dedee, pet," interposed Mrs. Jenny, "I hate that everlasting godmothering! I have already three round dozens of godchildren as surely as I stand here—*poor* people are not required for that purpose, I assure you. Come, I have finished here now, we will go to the nursery for awhile, or "—casting a glance at the old-fashioned clock—" still better, mamma has had some patterns for evening-dresses sent her—wait a minute and I will come up with you; the company won't come yet for an hour and a half."

She turned round gracefully once more as if to survey her work. The buffet shone with silver dishes, a bright fire burned in the open fireplace, the heavy chandelier as well as the sconces before the tall glass were filled with dark red twisted candles, and as Caroline drew back the heavy embroidered *portière*, a room almost too luxuriously furnished became visible—a room all crimson ; even through the stained glass of the bow-window the evening light sent red reflections in the labyrinth of chairs and sofas, lounges and tables, while white marble statues stood out against the dark green of costly greenhouse plants.

"It looks pleasant, doesn't it, Gertrude?" said the young wife. "I have not opened the great drawing-room because there will be only a few ladies. The wife of the Home Minister has accepted. Are you coming in for an hour?"

"No, thanks," replied the young girl, mounting the stairs with her sister to her mother's apartment. "Send me the baby for awhile, I like so much to have him."

"Oh, yes, the young gentleman shall make

his appearance," nodded Mrs. Jenny, "pro-
vided he doesn't sleep like a little dormouse."

"Do you go in to mamma," said Gertrude.
" I will change my dress and then come."

The rooms were the same as in the lower
story, also richly furnished, though not in the
new "æsthetic" style, yet they were not less elegant and comfortable. The sisters separated
in the ante-room, and Gertrude Baumhagen
went to her own room. She occupied the
room with the bow-window, but here the daylight was not broken by costly stained glass.
it came in, unhindered, in floods through
the clear panes, before which outside, number-
less flowers waved in the soft breeze. Directly
opposite were the gables of the Rathhaus;
like airy lace-work, the rich ornamentation of
the towers was marked out against the glowing evening sky.

This bow-window was a delightful place;
here stood her work-table, and behind it on an
easel, the portrait of the late Mr. Baumhagen.
The resemblance between the father and
daughter was visible at a glance; there was the
same light brown hair, the intellectual brow,
the small, fine nose, and the eyes too were the

same. She had always been his darling, and
it was her care that fresh flowers should
always be placed in the gold network of the
frame. And where she sat at work her hands
would sometimes rest in her lap and her eyes
would turn to the picture. " My dear, good
papa ! " she would whisper then, as if he must
understand.

To-day also, she walked quickly towards the
bow-window and looked long at the picture.
" You would have done that too," she said,
softly, " wouldn't you, papa ? " An earnest expression came suddenly into the young eyes,
something like inexpressible longing. " No,
every one is not like mamma and Jenny ; there
are warm human hearts, there are hearts that
feel compassion for a stranger's needs, for
whom the detested—" she stopped suddenly,
her small hands had clenched themselves and
her eyes filled with tears.

She began to pace up and down the room.
The soft, thick carpet deadened the sound of
her footsteps, but the heavy silk rustled after
her with an anxious sound.

What humiliations she had to endure daily
and hourly from the fact of being a rich girl !

She owed everything to the circumstance of having a fortune. Jenny had just now declared to her again that she had only been godmother, because—Ah, no matter, she knew better. Johanna was too modest. But she had not yet recovered from that other blow. A week ago there had been manœuvres in the neighborhood, and the colonel with his adjutant had had his quarters for two days in the Baumhagen house. She could not really remember that she had spoken more than a few commonplace words to the adjutant, and twenty-four hours after the troops had left the city—yesterday—a letter lay before her filled with the most ardent protestations of love and an entreaty for her hand. She had taken the letter and gone to her mother with it, with the words: "Here is some one who wishes to marry my money. Will you write the answer, mamma? I cannot."

Now she was dreading the mention of this letter. She was not afraid that her mother would try to persuade her. No, no, she had always been independent enough not to order her life according to the will of another, but the matter would be discussed and the division between mother and daughter would only be made wider than ever.

She started; the door opened and her sister's voice called: "Do come, Gertrude, I can't make up my mind about that new red."

The young girl crossed the hall and a moment after stood in her mother's drawing-room, before her mother, a small woman with almost too rosy cheeks, and an exceedingly obstinate expression about the full mouth. She sat on the sofa beneath the large Swiss landscape, the work of a celebrated Düsseldorf master—Mrs. Baumhagen was fond of relating that she had paid five hundred dollars for it—and tossed about with her small hands, covered with diamonds, a mass of dress patterns.

"Gertrude," she cried, "this would do for you." And she held out a bit of blue silk. "It is a pity you are so different, it is so nice for two sisters to dress alike."

"What is suitable for a married woman, is not fit for a girl," declared Mrs. Jenny. "Gertrude ought to get married, she is twenty years old."

"Ah! that reminds me,"—the mother had

3

been turning over the patterns during the conversation,—"there is that letter from your last
admirer, I must answer it. What am I to
write him?—

"See here, Jenny, this brown ground with
the blue spots is pretty, isn't it?—It is really
a great bore to answer letters like that; why
don't you do it yourself?"

"I am afraid my answer would not be dis-
passionate enough," replied the girl, calmly.

"Do you like him?" asked her sister.

The young girl ignored the question.

"I am afraid I might be bitter, and nothing
is required but a purely business-like answer,
as the question was purely one of business."

"You are delicious!" laughed the young
wife. "O what a pity you had not lived in
the middle ages, when the knights were
obliged to go through so long a probation!
Little goose, you must learn to take the world
as it is. Do you suppose Arthur would have
married *me* if I had had nothing? I assure
you he would never have thought of it! And
do you suppose I would have taken *him* if I
had not known he was in good circumstances?
Never! And what would you have more

from us? we are a comparatively happy couple."

Gertrude looked at her sister in surprise, with a questioning look in her blue eyes.

"Comparatively happy?" she repeated in a low tone.

"Good gracious, yes, he has his whims— one has to put up with them," declared her sister.

"Pray don't quarrel to-day," said Mrs. Baumhagen, taking her eye-glass from her snub-nose; "besides I will write the letter. It is for that I am your mother." She sighed.

"But in this matter I think Jenny is right. Gertrude, you take far too ideal views of the world. We have all seen to what such ideas lead." Another sigh. "I will not try to persuade you, I did not say anything to influence Jenny; you both know that very well. For my own part I have nothing against this Mr. Mr.—Mr.—" the name did not occur to her at once.

The young girl laughed, but her eyes looked scornful. "His address is given with great distinctness in the letter," she said.

"There is no great hurry, I suppose," continued her mother. "I have my whist-party this evening; if I am not there punctually I must pay a fine; besides, I don't feel like writing." She yawned slightly.

"The evenings are getting very long now—did you know, Jenny, that an opera troupe is coming here?"

Jenny answered in the affirmative, and added that she must go and dress.

"Good night," she cried, merrily, from the door; "we shall not meet again to-day."

"Good night, mamma," said Gertrude also.

"Are you going down to Jenny?" asked Mrs. Baumhagen.

The girl shook her head.

"What are you going to do all the evening?"

"I don't know, mamma. I have all sorts of things to do. Perhaps I shall read."

"Ah! Well, good night, my child."

She waved her hand and Gertrude went away. She took off her silk dress when she reached her room and exchanged it for a soft cashmere, then she went into her pretty sitting-room. It was already twilight and the lamps were being lighted in the street below.

She stood in the bow-window and watched one flame leap out after the other and the windows of the houses brighten. Even the old apple-woman, under the shelter of the statue of Roland, hung out her lantern under her gigantic white umbrella. Gertrude knew all this so well; it had been just the same when she was a tiny girl, and there was no change—only here inside it was all so different —so utterly different.

Where were those happy evenings when she had sat here beside her father—where was the old comfort and happiness? They must have hidden themselves away in his coffin, for ever since that dreadful day when they had carried her father away, it had been cold and empty in the house and in the young girl's heart. He had been so ill, so melancholy; it was fortunate that it had happened, so people said to the widow, who was almost wild in her passionate grief, but she had gone on a journey at once with Jenny, and had spent the winter in Nice. Gertrude would not go with them on any account. Her eyes, which had looked on such misery, could not look out upon God's laughing world,—her shattered

nerves could not bear the gay whirl of such a
life. She had stayed behind with an old aunt
—Aunt Louise slept almost all day, when
she was not eating or drinking coffee, and the
young girl had learned all the horrors of loneliness. She had been ill in body and mind,
and when her mother and sister had returned,
she learned that one may be lonely even in
company, and lonely she had remained until
the present day.

Urged by a longing for affection, she had
again and again tried to find excuses for her
mother, and to adapt herself to her mode of
life. She had allowed herself to be drawn
into the whirl of pleasure into which the
pleasure-loving woman had plunged so soon
as her time of mourning was over. She had
tried to persuade herself that concerts, balls,
and all the gayeties of society really gave
her pleasure and satisfied her. But her sense
of right rebelled against this self-deception.
She began to ponder on the vacuity of all
about her, on this and that conversation, on
the whole whirl around her, and she grew less
able to comprehend it. She could not understand how people could find so much amuse-

ment in things that seemed to her not worth a
thought. The art of fluttering through life,
skimming the cream of all its excitements as
Jenny did, she did not understand. To wear
the most elegant costume at a ball, to stay at
the dearest hotels on a journey, to be celebrated for giving the finest dinners—all that
was not worth thinking about. Once she had
asked if she might not read aloud in the evenings they spent alone, as she used to do when
her father was alive. After receiving permission she had come in with a radiant face,
bringing "Ekkehard," the last book which
her father had given her. With flushed
cheeks and sparkling eyes, she had read on
and on, but as she chanced to look up there
sat Jenny, looking through the last number of the "Journal of Fashion," while her
mother was sound asleep. She did not say a
word but she never read aloud again.

The large tears ran suddenly down her
cheeks. One of those moments had suddenly
come over her again, when she stretched out
her arms despairingly after some human soul
that would understand her, that would love
her a little, only a little, for herself alone. She

had grown so distrustful that she ascribed all kindness from strangers to her wealth and the position which her family held in society. She was quite conscious that she was repellent and unamiable, designedly so—no one should know how poor she really felt. It was not necessary for them to know that she wrung her hands and asked, "What shall I do? What do I live for?" She had inherited from her father a delight in work, a need for being of use—every responsible person feels a desire to be happy and to make others happy—but she felt her life so great a burden, it was so shallow, so distasteful, so full of petty interests.

She quickly dried her tears and turned; the door had opened and an old servant entered.

"You are forgetting your tea again, Miss Gertrude," she began, reproachfully. "It is all ready in the dining-room. I have brought in the tea so it will cool a little, but you must come now."

The young girl thanked her pleasantly and followed her. She returned in a very short time, nothing tasted good when she was so alone. She lighted the lamp and took a book and read. It had grown still gradually outside in the street, quarter after quarter struck from St. Benedict's tower, until it was eleven o'clock. A carriage drove up—her mother was coming home.

Gertrude closed her book, it was bedtime. The hall-door closed, steps went past Gertrude's door—but no, some one was coming in.

Mrs. Baumhagen still wore her black Spanish lace mantilla over her head. She only wished to ask her daughter what all this was about the christening this afternoon. The pastor's wife had told her a story of a curious kind of godfather; the pastor had come home full of it.

" Jenny did not come," explained the young girl, "and a strange gentleman offered to stand."

"But how horribly pushing " cried the excited little woman. "You should have drawn back, child—who knows what sort of a person he may be."

" I don't know him, mamma. But whoever he may be, he was so very good; he never supposed, I am sure, that his kindness could be misunderstood."

"There," cried Mrs. Baumhagen, "you see it is always so with you—you are so easily imposed upon by that sort of thing, Gertrude, —really I get very anxious about you. Did you know that Baron von Löwenberg—I remember the name now—is a distant connection of the ducal house of A.? Mrs. von S—— knows the whole family, they are charming people. But I will not influence you, I am only telling you this by the way. Sophie tells me an invitation has come from the Stadt-räthin for to-morrow. One never has a day to one's self. You will come too? It is about the Society festival; you young girls will have something to do.

"Jenny had a light still," she continued, without noticing her daughter's silence. "Arthur brought home Carl Röben, who came for his young wife, and Lina was just coming up out of the cellar with champagne.—I beg you will not tell any one about that scene in the church to-day; I have asked the pastor's wife to be silent too.

"Good night, my child. Of course the tea wasn't fit to drink at Mrs. S—— as usual."

"Good-night, mamma," replied Gertrude. She took the lamp and looked at her father's picture once more, then she went to bed. She awoke suddenly out of a half-slumber; she had heard the voice so distinctly that she had heard in the church to-day for the first time. She sat up with her heart beating quickly. No, what she had experienced to-day had been no dream. Like a ray of sunshine fell that friendly act of the unknown into this world of egotism and heartlessness. And then she staid long awake.

CHAPTER III.

THE storms of late autumn came on among the mountains, heavy showers of rain came down from the gray flying clouds and beat upon the dead leaves of the forest and against the windows of the dwelling-houses. Frank Linden sat at his writing-table in the room he had fitted up for himself in the second story, and his eyes wandered from the denuded branches in the garden to the mountains opposite. His surroundings were as comfortable as it is possible for a bachelor's room to be—books and weapons, a bright fire in the stove, good pictures on the walls, the delicate perfume of a fine cigar, and yet in spite of all this the expression on his handsome face was by no means a contented one.

He thrust aside a great sheet full of figures and took up instead a sheet of writing-paper, on which he began rapidly to write :—

44

" My Dear Old Judge :

" How you would scoff at me if you could see me in my present downcast mood. It is raining outside, and inside a flood of vexatious thoughts is streaming over me. I have found out that playing at farming is a pleasure only when one has a large purse that he can call his own. The expenses are getting too much for me ; everything has to be repaired or renewed. Well, all this is true, but I do not complain, for in other ways I have the greatest pleasure out of it. I cannot describe to you how really poetic a walk through these autumn woods is, which I manage to take almost daily with old Juno, thanks to the permission of the royal forester, with whom I have made friends

" And how delightful is the home coming beneath my own roof!

"But you, most prosaic of all mortals, are probably thinking only about venison steaks or broiled field-fares, and you only know the mood of the wild huntsman from hearsay.

" But I wanted to tell you how right you were when you declared of Wolff : ' *Hic niger est!* Be on your guard against this man—he is a scoundrel ! ' Perhaps that would be saying too much, but at any rate he is troublesome. He sent me yesterday a ticket to a concert and wrote on a bit of paper : ' Seats 38 to 40 taken by the Baumhagen family—I got No. 37.' Then he added that the Baumhagens

were the most distinguished and the wealth-
iest of the patricians in the city—evidently
those who play first fiddle there.

" You know what my opinion is concerning
millionaires—anything to escape their neighborhood.

" Well, in short, I was vexed and sent him
back the ticket with the remark that I was the
most unmusical person in the world.　He has
already made several attacks of that nature
on me, so I suppose there must be a daughter.

" And now to come at length to the aim of
this letter—you know that Wolff has a heavy
mortgage on Niendorf, at a very high rate of
interest.　I simply cannot pay it, and wish to
take up the mortgage ; would your sister be
willing to take it at a moderate rate?　I am
ready to give you any information.

" And what more shall I tell you?　By the
way, the old aunt—you did her great injus-
tice ; I never saw a more inoffensive, more
contented creature than this old woman.　A
niece who comes to Niendorf every year on a
visit, and whom she seems very fond of, her
tame goldfinch, and her artificial flowers
make up her whole world.　She asked quite
anxiously if I would let her have her room
here till she died.　I promised it faithfully.
She has been telling me a good many things
about my uncle's last years.　He must have

been very eccentric. Wolff was with him every day, playing euchre with him and the schoolmaster. He died at the card-table, so to speak. The old lady told me in a sepulchral voice that he actually died with clubs and diamonds in his hands. He had just played out the ace and said, ' There is a bomb for you !' and it was all over. I believe she felt a little horror of this ending, herself. I am going now into the city in spite of wind and rain to make a few calls. I have got to do it sooner or later. I shall take the steward with me ; he will bring home a pair of farm-horses that he bought the other day. Perhaps I may happen to stumble on my unknown little godmother that I wrote you about the other day ; so far luck has not favored me."

He added greetings and his signature, and half an hour later he was on his way to the city in faultless visiting costume.

Arrived in the hotel he inquired for a number of addresses, then began with a sigh to do his duty according to that extraordinary custom which Mrs. Grundy prescribes as necessary in " good society," that is, to call upon perfect strangers at mid-day and exchange a few shallow phrases and then to escape **as**

quickly as possible. Thank Heaven! No
one was at home to-day although it was raining in torrents. From a sort of natural opposition he left the Baumhagens to the last; he
belonged to that class to whom it is only necessary to praise a thing greatly in order to
create a strong dislike to it.

Just as he was on the point of making this
visit, he met Mr. Wolff. "You are going to
the Baumhagens?" he asked, evidently agreeably surprised. "There—there, that house
with the bow-window. I wish you good luck,
Mr. Linden!"

Frank had a sharp answer on his lips but
the little man had disappeared. But a
woman's figure stepped back hastily from the
bow-window above him.

"Very sorry," said the old servant-maid.
"Mrs. Baumhagen is not at home." He received the same answer in the lower story
although he heard the sounds of a Chopin
waltz.

He heard an explanation of this in the
hotel at dinner. A great ball was to take
place that evening, and such a festival natu-
rally required the most extensive preparations

on the part of the feminine portion of society ; on such a day neither matron nor maiden was visible. Nothing else was spoken of but this ball, and some of the gentlemen kindly invited him to be present; he would find some pretty girls there.

"I am curious to know if the little Baumhagen will be there," said an officer of Hussars.

"She may stay away for all I care," responded a very blond Referendary. "She has a way of condescending to one that I can't endure. She is perfectly eaten up with pride."

"She has just refused another offer, as I heard from Arthur Fredericks," cried another.

"She is probably waiting for a prince," snarled a fourth.

"I don't care," said Colonel von Brelow, "you may say what you like, she is a magnificent creature without a particle of provincialism about her. There is race in the girl."

Frank Linden had listened with an interest which had almost awakened a desire in him to take part in the ball. He half promised to appear, took the address of a glove-shop and

4

sat for a couple of hours in lively conversation.   After the lonely weeks he had been
spending it interested him more than he was
willing to confess.

"I am really stooping to gossip," he said,
amused at himself.   When he went out into
the street, darkness had already come down on
the short November day, the gas-lamps were
reflected back from the pools in the street, the
shop-windows were brilliantly lighted, and five
long strokes sounded from the tower of St.
Benedict's.

He went round the corner of the hotel into
the next street, and walked slowly along on
the narrow sidewalk, looking at the shops
which were all adorned with everything gay
and brilliant for the approaching Christmas
holidays.

"Good-evening!" said suddenly a timid
voice behind him.   He turned round.   For a
moment he could not remember the woman
who stood timidly before him, with a yoke on
her shoulder from which hung two shining
pails.   Then he recognized her—it was Johanna.

"I only wanted to thank you so

much," she began, "the sexton brought me the present for the baby."

"And is my little godchild well?" he asked, walking beside the woman and suddenly resolving to learn something about "her" at any price.

"Oh, thank you, Mr. Linden; it is but a weakly thing—trouble hasn't been good for him. But if the gentleman would like to see him—it isn't so very far and I'm going straight home now."

"Of course I should," he said, and learned as he went along, that she carried milk twice a day for a farmer's wife.

"Does the young lady come to see her godson sometimes?"

"Ay, to be sure!" replied the woman. "She comes and the baby hasn't a frock or a petticoat that she hasn't given him. She is so good, Miss Gertrude. We were confirmed together," she added, with pride.

So her name was Gertrude.

They had still some distance to go, through narrow streets and alleys, before the woman announced that they had reached her house. "There is a light inside—perhaps it is mother, the child waked up I suppose. My mother lives up stairs," she explained, " my father is a shoemaker."

The window was so low that a child might have looked in easily, so he could overlook the whole room without difficulty.

"Stay," he whispered, holding Johanna's arm.

"O goodness! it is the young lady," she cried, " I hope she won't be angry."

But Frank Linden did not reply. He saw only the slender girlish figure, as she walked up and down with the crying child in her arms, talking to him, dancing him till at last he stopped crying, looked solemnly in her face for awhile and then began to crow.

"Now you see, you silly little goosie," sounded the clear girl's voice in his ears, " you see who comes to take care of you when you were lying here all alone and all crumpled up, while your mother has to go out from house to house through all the wind and rain ; —you naughty baby, you little rogue, do you know your name yet? Let's see. Frank,— Frankie? O such a big boy! Now come here and don't cry a bit more and you shall

"SHE SAT DOWN BEFORE THE STOVE AND BEGAN TO TAKE OFF THE
LITTLE RED FLANNEL FROCK."

Page 53.

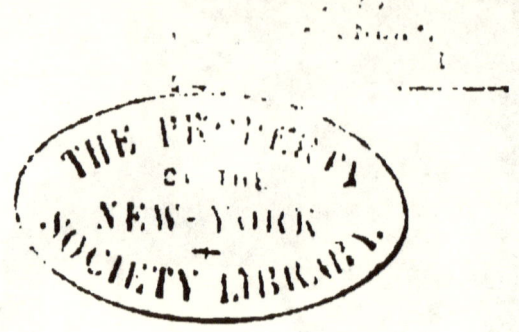

have on your warm little frock when your mother comes." And she sat down before the stove and began to take off the little red flannel frock.

"Ask if I may come in, Johanna," said Linden. And the next moment he had entered behind the woman.

A flush of embarrassment came over the young girl's face, but she frankly extended her hand. "I am glad to see you, Mr. Linden—mamma was very sorry that she could not receive you this afternoon. You—"

He bowed. Then she belonged to one of the houses where he had called to-day. But to which one?

"Do you know, I never knew till to-day that you were living in the neighborhood," she continued brightly. "I was standing in our bow-window when you came across the square, and saw you inquiring for our house."

"Then I have the honor to see Miss Baumhagen?" he asked, somewhat disturbed by this information.

"Gertrude Baumhagen," she replied. 'Why do you look so surprised?"

With these words she took her cloak from

the nearest chair, put a small fur cap on her brown hair and took up her muff.

"I must go now, Johanna, but I will send the doctor to-morrow for the baby. You must not let things go so,—you must take better care or else he may have weak eyes all his life."

"Will you allow me to accompany you?" asked Linden, unable to take his eyes off the graceful form. And that was Gertrude Baum-hagen!

She assented. "I am not afraid for myself, but I am sure you would never find your way out of this maze of streets into which my good Johanna has enticed you. This part about here is quite the oldest part of the town. You cannot see it this evening, but by daylight a walk through this quarter would well repay you. I like this neighborhood, though only people of the lower class live here," she continued, walking with a firm step on the slippery pavement.

"Do you see down there on the corner that house with the great stone steps in front and the bench under the tree? My grandmother was born in that house, and the tree is a Span-

ish lilac.   Grandfather fell in love with her as
she sat one evening under the tree rocking
her youngest brother.   She has often told me
about it.   The lilac was in blossom and she
was just eighteen.   Isn't it a perfect little
poem ? "

Then she laughed softly.   " But I am telling you all this and I don't know in the least
what you think of such things."

They were just opposite the small house
with the lilac tree.   He stopped and looked
up.   She perceived it and said : " I   can
never go by without having happy thoughts
and pleasant memories.   Never was there a
dearer grandmother, she was so simple and
so good."   And as he was silent she added,
as if in explanation, " She was a granddaugh-
ter of the foreman in grandpapa's factory."

Still nothing occurred to him to say and he
could not utter a merely conventional phrase.

She too remained silent for a while.
" May I ask you," she then began, " not to
give too many presents to the baby—they are
simple people who might be easily spoiled."

He assented.   " A man like me is so un-
practical," he said, by way of excuse.   " I

did not exactly know what was expected of me after I had offered myself as godfather in such an intrusive manner."

"That was no intrusion, that was a feeling of humanity, Mr. Linden."

"I was afraid I might have seemed to you, too impulsive—too—" he stopped.

"O no, no," she interrupted earnestly. "What can you think of me? I can easily tell the true from the false—I was really very glad," she added, with some hesitation.

"I thank you," he said.

And then they walked on in silence through the streets;—Gertrude Baumhagen stopped before a flower-store behind whose great glass panes a wealth of roses, violets and camellias glowed.

"Our ways separate here," she said, as she gave him her hand. "I have something to do in here. Good-bye, Mr.—Godfather."

He had lifted his hat and taken her hand. "Good-bye, Miss Baumhagen." And hesitatingly he asked—"Shall you be at the ball to-night?"

"Yes," she nodded, "at the request of the higher powers," and her blue eyes rested quietly on his face. There was nothing of youthful pleasure and joyful expectation to be read in them. " Mamma would have been in despair if I had declined. Good-night, Mr. Linden."

. The young man stood outside as she disappeared into the shop. He stood still for a moment, then he went on his way.

So that was Gertrude Baumhagen! He really. regretted that that was her name, for he had taken a prejudice against the name, which he had associated with vulgar purse-pride. The conversation at the hotel table recurred to him. He had figured to himself a supercilious blonde who used her privileges as a Baumhagen and the richest girl in the city, to subject her admirers to all manner of caprices. And he had found the Gertrude of the church, a lovely, slender girl, with a simple unspoiled nature, possessing no other pride than that of a noble woman.

Involuntarily he walked faster. He would accept the kind invitation to the ball. But when he reached the hotel he had changed his mind again. He did not care to see her as a modern society woman, he would not efface that lovely picture he had seen through the window of that poor little house. He could not have borne it if she had met him in the brilliant ball-room, with that air of condescension with which he had heard her reproached to-day. He decided to dine at home.

With this thought he had walked down the street again till he reached the flower-shop. On a sudden impulse he entered and asked for a simple bouquet.

The woman had an immense bouquet in her hand at the moment, resembling a cart-wheel surrounded by rich lace, which she was just giving to the errand-boy.

"For Miss Baumhagen," she said, "here is the card."

Frank Linden saw a coat-of-arms over the name. He stepped back a moment, undecided what to do. Then the shopwoman turned towards him.

"A simple bouquet," he repeated. There was none ready, but they could make up one immediately. The young man himself chose the flowers from the wet sand and gave them to her. It must have been a pleasant occu-

pation for he was constantly putting back a
rose and substituting a finer one for it. At
last it was finished, a graceful bouquet of
white roses just tinted with pink, like a
maiden's blush, interspersed with maiden-hair
and delicate ferns. He looked at the dainty
blossoms once more, then paid for it and
went back to the hotel. Then he laid the
bouquet on the table, called for ink and
paper, took a visiting-card and wrote. Suddenly he stopped and smiled, "What nonsense!" he said, half aloud, "she is sure
to carry the big bouquet." Then he began
again and read it over. It was a little verse
asking if the godfather might at this late hour
send to the godmother the flowers which
according to ancient custom he ought to have
offered at the christening, and modestly hop-
ing she would honor them by carrying them
to the ball that night. He smiled again, put
it into the envelope and gave the bouquet
and letter to a messenger with instructions to
carry both to Miss Baumhagen. And then
a thought struck him—the ball began at eight
o'clock—that would be in ten minutes—he
would see Gertrude Baumhagen, see—if his

bouquet—nonsense! Very likely! But then he would wait. "It is well the judge does not see me now!" he whispered to himself. He felt like a child at Christmas time, so happy was he and so full of expectation as he wandered up and down the square in front of the hotel.

CHAPTER IV.

THE clock struck eight. Gentlemen on foot had already been coming to the hotel for some time, then ladies arrived, and at length the first carriage containing guests for the ball rolled up, dainty feet tripped up the steps, and rich silks rustled as they walked. Carriage followed carriage; now came an elegant equipage with magnificent gray horses, a charming slight woman's figure in a light blue dress covered with delicate lace, bent forward, and a silvery laugh sounded in Linden's ear. "It is Mrs. Fredericks," he heard the people murmur behind him.

So that was her sister!

The beautiful young wife swept up the steps like a lovely fairy, followed by her husband in a faultless black dress-coat, carrying her fan and bouquet.

The carriage dashed across the market-

place again, to return in less than five minutes.

"Gertrude!" whispered Linden, drawing
involuntarily further back into the shadow.
A short stout lady in a light gray dress
descended from the carriage, then *she* glided
out and stood beside her mother, slender and
graceful in her shimmering white silk, her
beautiful shoulders lightly covered, and in her
hand a well-known bouquet of pale roses.
But this was not the girl of a few hours back.
The small head was bent back as if the massive light brown braids were too heavy for it,
and an expression of proud reserve which he
had not before perceived, rested on the open
countenance.

Two gentlemen started forward to greet
the ladies ; the first gallantly offered his arm
to the mother, the other approached the young
girl.   She thanked him proudly, scarcely touching his arm with her finger-tips.   Then suddenly this figure from which he could not
take his eyes, vanished like a beautiful vision.

The encounter had left him in a mood of
intense excitement.   He bestowed a dollar
on a poor woman who stood beside him

with a miserable child in her arms, and he ordered out so big a glass of hot wine for old Summerfeld, his coachman, that the old man was alarmed and hoped " they should get . home all right."

" What folly it is," said Linden to himself. And when a moment later his carriage drove up, and at the same moment the notes of a Strauss waltz struck his ear, he began to hum the air of "The Rose of the South." Then the carriage rattled over the market-place out on the dark country road, and sooner than usual he was at home in his quiet little room, taking a thousand pleasant thoughts with him.

In the manor-house at Niendorf there was one room in which roses bloomed in masses ; not only in the boxes between the double windows or in the pots on the sill according to the season, but in the room itself, thousands of earth's fairest flowers were wreathed about the pictures and furniture. It had a strange effect, especially when instead of the sleeping beauty one might have expected to find here, one perceived a very old woman in an arm chair by the window, unweariedly engaged

in cutting leaves and petals out of colored
silk paper, shaping and putting them together so that at length a rose trembled on its
wire stem, looking as natural from a little
distance as if it had just been cut from the
bush. Aunt Rosalie could not live without
making roses; she lavished half her modest
income on silk paper, and every one whom she
wished well, received a wreath of roses as a
present, red, pink, white and yellow blossoms
tastefully intermixed. All the village beauties
wore roses of Aunt Rosalie's manufacture in
their well-oiled hair at the village dances.
The graves in the church-yard displayed
masses of white and crimson roses from the
same store, torn and faded by wind and sun.
The little church was lavishly decked every
year by Aunt Rosalie, with these witnesses to
her skill.

She was known therefore throughout the
village to young and old as " Aunt Rose " or
" Miss Rose," and not seldom was she followed
in her walks by a crowd of children, especially little girls, with the petition " a rose for
for me too ! " And " Aunt Rose " was always
prepared for them ; the less successful speci-

mens were kept entirely for this purpose and were distributed from her capacious reticule with a lavish hand.

Frank Linden had long been accustomed to spend an occasional hour in the old lady's society. At the sight of her something of the atmosphere of peace which surrounded her seemed to descend upon him and calmed and soothed him. She would sit calm and still at her little table, her small withered hands busied in forming the "symbols of a well-rounded life." By degrees she had related to him in a quaintly solemn tone, stories of the lives which had passed under the pointed gables of this roof. There was little light and much shade among them, much guilt, and error, a dark bit of life-history. A married pair who did not agree, an only child idolized by both, and this only son covered himself and his parents with disgrace and fled to America, where he died. The parents were left behind without hope or comfort in the world, each reproaching the other for the failure in their son's training. Then the wife died of grief, and now began an endless term of loneliness for the elderly man under a ban of misanthropy

5

and scorn of his kind; loving no one but his dog, associating with no one except with Wolff, who brought the news and gossip of the town, and treating even him with a disdain bordering on insult.

"But you see, my dear nephew," the old aunt had added, "there are men who are more like hounds than the hounds themselves, —dogs will cry out when they are trodden upon, but the sort to which he belongs will smile humbly at the hardest kick—and William found such a man necessary to him."

It was snowing; the mountains were all white, the garden lay shrouded under a shining white coverlid, and white snow-flakes were dancing in the air. Frank Linden had come back from hunting with the steward, and after dinner he went into Aunt Rosalie's room. She rose as he entered and came towards him.

"There you see, my dear nephew, what happens when you go out for a day. You have had a visit, such a splendid fashionable visitor in a magnificent sleigh. I was just taking my walk in the corridor as he came up

the stairs and here is his card,"—she searched in her reticule—" which he left for you."

Frank took the card and read. " Arthur Fredericks." " Oh, I am sorry," he said, really regretting his loss. " When was he here ? "

" Oh, just at noon precisely, when most Christians are eating their dinner," she replied. " And the postman has been here too and brought a letter for you. Oh, dear, where is it now ? Where could I have put it ? " And she turned about and began to look for it, first on the table among the pieces of silk paper and then on the floor, assisted by the young man.

" What did the letter look like, dearest Aunt ? "

" Blue—or gray—blue, I think," she replied, all out of breath, turning out the contents of her red silk reticule. She brought out a mass of rose-buds and an immense handkerchief edged with lace, but nothing else.

" Was the letter small or large ? " he inquired from behind the sofa.

" Large and thick," gasped Aunt Rosalie. " Such a thing never happened to me before in

my life—it is really dreadful." And with
astounding agility she turned over the things
on the consumptive little piano and tossed the
antique sheets of music about.

"Perhaps it got into the stove, Auntie."

"No, no, it has not been unscrewed since
this morning."

Frank Linden went to the bell and rung.
"Don't take any more trouble about it, Auntie,
the letter is sure to turn up; let the maid look
for it."

Dorothy came and looked, and looked
behind all the furniture, and shaking out all
the curtains—but in vain.

"Well, we will give it up," declared Linden
at length—"I suppose it is a letter from my
mother or from the Judge—I can ask them
what they had to say. Let us drink our
coffee, Auntie."

"I shan't sleep the whole night," declared
the little old lady in much excitement.

"O don't think any more about it," he
begged her, good-humoredly. "I am sure
there was nothing of any great importance in
it. Tell me some of your old stories now,
they will just suit this weather."

But the wrinkled face under the great cap still wore an anxious look, and the dim eyes kept straying away from the coffee cups searchingly round the room, lingering thoughtfully on the green lamp-shade. Evidently there was no hope of a conversation with her. After awhile the young man rose to go to his own room.

"Yes, go, go," she said, relieved, "and then I can think where I could have put that letter. Oh, my memory! my memory! I am growing so old."

He walked along the corridor and mounted the staircase into the second story. The twilight of the short winter day had already darkened all the corners. It was painfully still in the house, only the echo of his own footsteps sounding in his ear. It was such a day as his friend had predicted for him—horribly lonely and empty, it seemed to rest like a heavy weight on this world-remote house. One cannot always read, cannot always be busy, especially when the thoughts stray uneasily out over forest and meadow to a distinct goal, and always return anxious and doubting.

He stood in his room at the window and watched the snow flakes fluttering down in the darkening air, and fell into a dream as he had done every day for the last week. He gave himself up to it so entirely that he fancied he could distinctly hear a light step behind him on the carpet, and the soft tones of a woman's voice, saying, " Frank, Frankie ! " He turned and gazed into the dusky room. What if she were to open the door now,—what if she should come in with the child in her arms ? Why should it not be, why could it not be ? Were these walls not strong enough, these rooms not cosy and homelike enough to hold such happiness ?

He began to walk up and down. Folly ! Nonsense ! What was he thinking of ? Oh, if he had never come here, or better still if she were only the daughter of the foreman like her grandmother, and sat on the bench before the little house under the lilac tree, then everything would be so simple. He would not for the world enter that mad race for Gertrude Baumhagen's money-bags, in which so many had already come to grief. But her sweet friendship ?—

And then he fell helpless again before the charm of her eyes.

He was suffering from those doubts, from those alternating fears and hopes that torment every man who is in love. And Frank Linden in his loneliness had long since acknowledged to himself that he only wanted Gertrude Baumhagen to complete his happiness.

His was by no means a shy or retiring nature. On the contrary, he possessed that modest boldness which seems so natural to some people on whom society looks with favor. If he were owner of a large estate instead of this " hole "—as the Judge designated Niendorf—he would rather have asked to-day than to-morrow if she would be his wife, without too great a shyness of the money-bags. But as it was, he could not, he must make his way a little first, and before he could do that, who could tell what might have happened to Gertrude Baumhagen ?

He bit his lip at the thought—the result was always the same. But was a true heart nothing then, and a strong will ? If the Judge were only here so he could ask him—

During these thoughts he had lighted the
lamp.   There lay the card on the table, which
Aunt Rosalie had given him.   "Arthur
Fredericks."   He smiled as he thought of the
little insignificant man to whom her sister had
given her heart, and he could not think of
Gertrude as belonging to him in any way.
At last a return visit from him !   And there
were some half effaced words written with a
pencil.

"Very sorry not to have met you ; hope you
will come to a little supper at our house the
day after Christmas."

It was the first invitation to Gertrude's
house.   He wrote an acceptance at once.
Then he remembered that he had ordered the
sleigh to go to the city to do some errands
there.   He would send the hotel porter across
with the card.

CHAPTER V.

CHRISTMAS had passed and the last of the holidays had come with rain and thaw; it stripped off the brilliant white snowy coverlid from the earth as if it had been only a festal decoration, and the black earth was good enough for ordinary days.

Mrs. Baumhagen was sitting in a peevish mood at the window in her room looking out over the market-place. She had a slight headache, and besides—there was nothing at all to do to-day, no theatre, no party, not even the whist club, and yesterday at Jenny's it had been very dull. Finally she was vexed with Gertrude who, contrary to all custom, had talked eagerly to her neighbor at dinner, that stranger who had run after her in the church that time.

It was foolish of the children to have placed him beside her.

"A letter, Mrs. Baumhagen." Sophie brought in a simple white envelope.

"Without any post-mark? Who left it?" she asked, looking at the handwriting which was quite unknown to her.

"An old servant or coachman, I did not know him."

Mrs. Baumhagen shook her head as she took the letter and read it.

She rose suddenly, with a deep flush on her face, and called:

"Gertrude! Gertrude!"

The young girl came at once.

The active little woman had already rung the bell and said to Sophie as she entered:

"Call Mrs. Fredericks and my son-in-law, tell them to come quickly, quickly!—Gertrude, I must have an explanation of this. But I must collect myself first, must—"

"Mamma," entreated the young girl, turning slightly pale, "let us discuss the matter alone —why should Jenny and Arthur—?"

"Do you know then what is in this letter?" cried the excited mother.

"Yes," replied Gertrude, firmly, coming up

to the arm chair into which her mother had thrown herself.

" With your consent, child ?—Gertrude ? "

" With my consent, mamma," repeated the young girl, a clear, bright crimson staining the beautiful face.

Mrs. Baumhagen said not another word, but began to cry bitterly.

" When did you permit him to write to me ? " she asked, after a long pause, drying her eyes.

" Yesterday, mamma."

At this moment Jenny thrust her pretty blonde head in at the door.

" Jenny ! " cried the mother, the tears again starting to her eyes, and the obstinate lines about the mouth coming out more distinctly.

" For Heaven's sake, what is the matter ? " cried the young wife.

" Jenny, child ! Gertrude is engaged ! "

Mrs. Jenny recovered her composure at once. " Well," she cried, lightly, " is that so great a misfortune ? "

" But, to whom, to whom ! " cried the mother.

" Well ? " inquired Jenny.

" To that—that—yesterday—Linden is his

name, Frank Linden. Here it is down in black and white,—a man that I have hardly seen three times!"

Jenny turned her large and wondering eyes upon Gertrude, who was still standing behind her mother's chair.

"Good gracious, Gertrude," she cried, "what possessed you to think of him?"

"What possessed you to think of Arthur?" asked the young girl, straightening herself up. "How do people ever think of each other? I don't know, I only know that I love him, and I have pledged him my word."

"When, I should like to know?"

"Last evening, in your red room, Jenny.—if you think the *when* has anything to do with the matter."

"But, so suddenly, without any preparation. What guarantee have you that he—?"

"As good a guarantee at least," interrupted Gertrude, now pale to the lips, "as I should have had if I had accepted Lieutenant von Löwenberg's proposal the other day."

"Yes, yes, she is right there, mamma," said Jenny.

"Oh, of course!" was the reply, "I am to

say yes and amen at once. But I must speak to Arthur first and to Aunt Pauline and Uncle Henry. I will not take the responsibility of such a step on myself alone in any case."

" Mamma, you will not go asking the whole neighborhood," said the young girl, in a trembling voice. " It only concerns you and me, and—" she drew a long breath—" I shall hardly change my mind in consequence of any representations."

" But Arthur could make inquiries about him," interrupted Jenny.

" Thank you, Jenny, I beg you will spare yourself the trouble. My heart speaks loudly enough for him. If I had not known my own mind weeks ago, I should not be standing before you as I am now."

" You are an ungrateful and heartless child," sobbed her mother. " You think you will conquer me by your obstinacy. Your father used to drive me wild with just that same calmness. It makes me tremble all over only just to see those firmly closed lips and those calm eyes. It is dreadful !"

Gertrude remained standing a few minutes,

then without a word of reply she left the room.

" It is a speculation on his part," said Mrs. Jenny, carelessly, " there is no doubt of that."

" And she believes all he tells her," sobbed the mother. " That unlucky christening was the cause of it all. She is so impressed by anything of that sort."

Jenny nodded.

" And now she will just settle down forever at that wretched Niendorf, for there is no turning her when she has once made up her mind."

" Heaven forgive me, she has the Baumhagen obstinacy in full measure ; I know what I have suffered from it."

" This Linden is handsome," remarked Jenny, taking no notice of the violent weeping. " Goodness, what a stir it will make through the town ! She might have taken some one else. But did I not always tell you, mamma, that she was sure to do something foolish ? "

"Arthur ! " she cried to her husband who had just come in, " just fancy, Gertrude has engaged herself to that—Linden."

"The devil she has!" escaped Arthur Fredericks' lips.

" Tell me, my dear son, what do you know about him? You must have heard something at the Club, or—"

Mrs. Baumhagen had let her handkerchief fall, and was gazing with a look of woe at her son-in-law.

"Oh, he is a nice fellow enough, but poor as a church mouse. He knows what he is about when he makes up to Gertrude. Confound it! If I had known what he was up to, I would never have asked him here."

"Yes, and she declares she will not give him up," said Jenny.

" I believe that, without any assurances from you; she is your sister. When you have once got a thing into your head—well, I know what happens."

" Arthur!" sobbed the elder lady, reproachfully.

"I must beg, Arthur, that you will not always be charging me with spite and obstinacy," pouted the younger.

" But, my dear child, it is perfectly true—"

" Don't be always contradicting!" cried

Mrs. Jenny, energetically, stamping her foot and taking out her handkerchief, ready to cry at a moment's notice. He knew this manœuvre of old and drew his hand hastily through his hair.

"Very well then, what am I to do about it?" he asked. "What do you want of me?"

"Your advice, Arthur," groaned the mother-in-law.

"My advice? Well then—say yes."

"But he is so entirely without means, as I heard the other day," interposed Mrs. Baumhagen.

He shrugged his shoulders. "Bah! Gertrude can afford to marry a poor man. Besides—I don't know much about Niendorf, but I should think something might be made of it under good management. He seems to be the man for the place, and Wolff was telling me the other day that Linden was going to raise sheep on a large scale."

"That last bit of information of course settles the matter," remarked Jenny, ironically.

"No, no," cried the mother, sobbing again, "you none of you take it seriously enough. I cannot bring myself to consent, I have hardly

exchanged half a dozen words with this Linden.   Oh, what unheard-of presumption!"
She rose from her chair, and crimson with
excitement threw herself on the lounge.

"Now look out for hysterics," whispered
Arthur, indifferently, taking out a cigar.

Jenny answered only by a look, but that
was blighting. She took her train in her hand
and swept past her astonished husband.

"Take me with you," he said, gayly.

"Jenny, stay with me," cried her mother,
"don't leave me now."

And the young wife turned back, met her
husband at the door, and passed him with her
nose in the air to sit down beside her mother.

Oh, he had a long account to settle with
her; she would have her revenge yet for his
disagreeable remarks at the breakfast-table
when she quite innocently praised Colonel
von Brelow. He was not expecting anything
pleasant either; she could see that at once,
but only let him wait a little!

"How, mamma?" she inquired, "did you
think I had anything to say to Arthur? Bah!
He is an Othello—a blind one—they are always the worst."

6

"Ah, Jenny, that unhappy child—Gertrude."

"Oh, yes, to be sure," assented the young wife, " that stupid nonsense of Gertrude's—"

In the meantime the young girl was standing before her father's picture, her whole being in a tumult between happiness and pain. She had not closed her eyes the night before since she had shyly given him her hand with a scarcely whispered, "yes."

She knew he loved her; she had fancied a hundred times what it would be when he should tell her of it, and now it had come so suddenly, so unexpectedly. She had loved him long already, ever since she had seen him that first time; and since then she had escaped none of the joy and pain of a secret attachment.

She took nothing lightly, did nothing by halves, and she had given herself up wholly to this fascination. Whoever should try to take him from her now, must tear her heart out of her breast.

As she stood there the tears ran down over her pale face in great drops, but a smile lingered about the small pouting mouth.

"I know it very well," she whispered, nod-

ding at her father's picture, "you would be
sure to like him, papa!" And a happy memory of the words he had spoken yesterday
came back to her, of his lonely house, of his
longing for her, and that he could offer her
nothing but that modest home and a faithful
heart.

His only wealth at present was a multitude
of cares.

"Let me bear the cares with you, no happiness on earth would be greater than this," she
wished to say, but she had only drooped her
eyes and given him her hand—the words
would not pass her lips.

It was as if she had been walking in the
deepest shadow and had suddenly come out
into the warm, life-giving sunshine. "It is too
much, too much happiness!" she had thought
this morning when she got up. She thought
so still, and it seemed to her that the tears
she shed were only a just tribute to her overpowering happiness. If her mother had consented at once, if she had said, "He shall be
like a beloved son to me, bring him to me. at
once," that would have been too much, but
this refusal, this distrust seemed to be meant

to tone down her bliss a little. It was like the snow-storm in spring, which covers the early leaves and blossoms,—but when it is past do they not bloom out in double beauty?

The conversation in the next room grew more eager. Gertrude heard the complaining voice of her mother more clearly than before. It had a painful effect upon her and she cast a glance involuntarily at her father's picture, as if he could still hear what had been the torture of his life. Gertrude could recall so many scenes of complaint and crying in that very room. How often had her father's authoritative voice penetrated to her ear: "Very well, Ottilie, you shall have your way, but—spare me!" And how often had a pallid man entered through that door and thrown himself silently on the sofa as if he found a refuge here with his child. Ah, and it had been so too on that day, that dreadful day, when afterwards it had grown so still, so deathly still.

And there it was again, the loud weeping, the complaints against Heaven that had made her the most miserable of women, and now was punishing her through her children.

Then there was an opening and shutting of
doors, a running about of servants ; Gertrude
even fancied she could perceive the penetrat-
ing odor of valerian which Mrs. Baumhagen
was accustomed to take for her nervous attacks. And then the door flew open and
Jenny came in.

"Mamma is quite miserable," she said, reproachfully ; "I had to send for the doctor,
and Sophie is putting wet compresses on her
head. A lovely day, I must say !"

"I am so sorry, Jenny," said the young girl.

"Oh, yes, but it was a very sudden blow. I
must honestly confess that I cannot understand you, Gertrude. You must have refused
more than ten good offers, you were always so
fastidious, and now you have taken the first
best that offered."

"The best certainly," thought Gertrude, but
she was silent.

The young wife mistakenly considered this
as the effect of her words.

"Now just consider, child," she continued,
"think it over again, you—"

"Stop, Jenny," cried the young girl in a
firm voice. "What gives you the right to speak

so to me? Have I ever uttered a word about your choice? Did I not welcome Arthur kindly? What advantages has he over Linden? I alone have to judge as to the wisdom of this step, for I alone must bear the consequences. It is not right to try to influence a person in a matter that is so individual, that so entirely concerns that person alone."

"Good gracious, don't get so excited about it!" cried Jenny. "We do not consider him an eligible *parti*, because he is entirely without fortune."

A deep shadow passed over Gertrude's pale face. "Oh, put aside the question of money," she entreated; "do not disturb the sweetest dream of my life—don't speak of it, Jenny."

But Jenny continued—"No, I will not keep silent, for you live in dreamland, and you must look a little at the realities of life that you may not fall too suddenly out of your fancied heaven. Perhaps you imagine that Frank Linden would have shown such haste if you had not been Gertrude Baumhagen? Most certainly he would not! I consider it my duty to tell you that mamma, as well as Arthur and I, are of the opinion that his first thought was of the capital our good father—" She stopped, for Gertrude stood before her, tall and threatening.

"You may comfort yourself, Jenny," she gasped out. "I believe in him, and I shall speak no word in his defence. You and the others may think what you please, I cannot prevent it, cannot even resent it, you—" She stopped, she would not utter the bitter words. —"Be so kind as to tell mamma that I will not break my word to him." She added, more calmly, "I shall be so grateful to you, Jenny—if any one can do anything with her it is you—her darling!"

CHAPTER VI.

THE young wife left her sister's room almost in consternation. She could find nothing to say to Gertrude's unexpected reliance upon her. The sisters had never understood each other. Jenny could not comprehend now how any one could be so blinded and so unwise, and she was startled as if by something pure and lofty as the clear girlish eyes rested on her, which could still discover poetry amid all the dusty prose of life. She sat down again beside the sofa.

"Mamma," she whispered, after a pause, during which she balanced her small slipper thoughtfully on the tip of her toe, "Mamma, I really believe you can't help it—will you have a little eau de cologne?—Gertrude is so madly in love with him. I am sure you will have to give your consent, notwithstanding it is so great a disappointment."

Gertrude remained standing in the middle of the room looking after her sister. She felt sorry for her. It must be dreadful when one could no longer believe in love and disinterestedness, and the image of Frank Linden's true eyes rose up before her as clear as his pure heart itself. Can a man look like that with ulterior motives? can a man speak so with a lie in his heart? She could have laughed aloud in her blissful certainty. Even though she were poor, a beggar indeed, he would still love her.

In the afternoon a great conference was held. At twelve o'clock an order was suddenly given from the sofa to have the drawing-room heated, the Dresden coffee service taken out, and some cakes sent for from the confectioner's. Madame Ottilie would hold a family counsel.

The aroma of Sophie's celebrated coffee penetrated even to Gertrude's lonely room. She could hear the doors open and shut, and now and then the voice of Aunt Pauline, and Uncle Henry's comfortable laugh. The day drew near its close and still no conclusion seemed to have been arrived at, but Gertrude

sat calmly in her bow-window and waited.
He would be calm too, she was sure of that—
he had her word. Steps at last—that must
be her uncle.

"Well, Miss Gertrude !" he called out into
the dusky room—"he came, he saw, he
conquered—eh? Fine doings, these. Your
mother is in a pretty temper over the presumption of the bold youth. He will need all
his fascinations to gain her favor as a mother-
in-law. Well, come in now, and thank me for
her consent."

"I knew it, uncle," she said, pleasantly.
"I was sure you would stand by me."

He was a little old gentleman with a little
round body, which he always fed well in his
splendid bachelor dinners; always in good
humor, especially after a good glass of wine.
And as he knew what an agreeable effect this
always had upon him, he never failed for the
benefit of mankind, to make use of this means
of making himself amiable and merry. He
now took the tall, slender girl laughingly by
the hand as if she were a child, and led her
towards the door.

"Live and let live, Gertrude ! " he cried.

"It is out of pure egotism that I made such a commotion about it. You need not thank me, I was only joking. You see, I can stand anything but a scene and a woman's tears, and your mother understands that sort of thing to a T. That always upsets me you know. 'Don't make a fuss, Ottilie,' I said. 'Why shouldn't the little one marry that handsome young fellow? You Baumhagen girls are lucky enough to be able to take a man simply because you like him.' Ta, ta! Here comes the bride!" he called out, letting Gertrude pass before him into the lighted room.

She walked with a light step and a grave face up to her mother, who was reclining in the corner of the sofa as if she were entirely worn out by the important discussion. By her side sat the thin aunt in a black silk dress, her blond cap reposing on her brown false front, in full consciousness of her dignity. Jenny sat near her while Arthur was standing by the stove. The ladies had been drinking coffee, the gentlemen wine. The violet velvet curtains were drawn and everything looked cosy and comfortable.

"I thank you, mamma," said Gertrude.

Mrs. Baumhagen nodded slightly and touched her daughter's lips with hers. "May you never repent this step," she said, faintly; "it is not without great anxiety that I give my consent, and I have yielded only in consequence of my knowledge of your unbending— yes, I must say it now—passionate character —and for the sake of peace."

A bitter smile played about Gertrude's mouth.

"I thank you, mamma," she repeated.

"My dear Gertrude," began her aunt, solemnly, "take from me too—"

"Oh, come," interposed Uncle Henry, very ungallantly, "do have compassion, in the first place on me, but next on that languishing youth in Niendorf, and send him his answer. It has happened before now that dreadful consequences have followed such suspense; I could tell you some blood-curdling stories about it, I assure you. Come, we will write out a telegram," he continued, drawing a note-book from his pocket and tearing out a leaf, while he borrowed a pencil from his dear nephew Arthur.

"Well, what shall it be, Gertrude?" he in-

quired, when he was ready to write. ' Come to
my arms !' or ' Thine forever !' or ' Speak
to my mother,' or—ha ! ha ! I have it—' My
mother will see you ; come to-morrow and get
her consent. Gertrude Baumhagen.' ' And
get her consent,' " he spelt out as he wrote.

"Thanks, uncle," said the young girl ; " I
would rather write it myself in my room ; his
coachman is waiting at the hotel opposite."

She could hear her uncle's hearty laugh
over the poor fellow who had been sighing in
suspense from eleven o'clock this morning till
now, and then she shut her door. With a
trembling hand she lighted her lamp and
wrote : " Mamma has consented ; I shall expect you to-morrow. Your Gertrude."

The old Sophie, who had been a servant in
the Baumhagen house before the master was
married, took the note. " I will carry it across
myself, Miss Gertrude," she said, "and if
it was pouring harder than it is, and if I got
my rheumatism back for it, I would go all the
same. I have the fate of two people in my
hand in this little bit of paper. God grant
that it may bring joy to you both, Miss
Gertrude."

Gertrude pressed her hand and then went to the bow-window and looked through the glass to watch Sophie as she crossed the square. Her white apron fluttered now under the street-lamp near the old apple-woman, and then under the swinging lamp before the hotel. If the old man would only drive as fast as his horses could carry him! Every minute of waiting seemed too long to her now.

Then the white apron appeared again under the hotel lamp, but there was somebody before it. Gertrude pressed her hands suddenly against her beating heart. "Frank!" she gasped, and her limbs almost refused to support her as she tried to make a few steps. He had waited for the answer himself!

"There he is, there he is, my bridegroom!" escaped from the quivering lips. The whole sacred signification of that blessed word overpowered her. Then Sophie opened the door softly and he crossed the threshold of the dainty maiden's boudoir, and shut the door as softly behind him. The faithful old servant could only see how her proud young mistress nestled into his arms and mutely received his kisses—"Oh, what a wonderful thing this love is!" she said, smiling to herself.

Then she turned towards the drawing-room, but when she reached the door she turned away with a shake of her head. They would all be rushing in and she would not shorten these blessed minutes for Gertrude. It would be time enough to go to "madam" in a quarter of an hour. And she busied herself in the corridor in order to be at hand at the right moment, in case they should both forget all about the mother in the multiplicity of things they had to say.

It was midnight before Linden finally drove home. The jovial uncle had gotten up a little celebration of the betrothal on the spur of the moment, and made a long speech himself. Then Mrs. Jenny had been very gay and had laughed and jested with her brother-in-law *in spe.* But Mrs. Baumhagen, after a private interview of half an hour with the young man, remained silent and grave, and played out her rôle of anxious mother to the end. She scarcely touched her lips to the glass of champagne when the company drank to the health of the young betrothed.

Frank Linden, however, had not taken offence at her coldness. She knew him so slightly, and he had come like a hungry wolf to rob her of her one little lamb.

It must be dreadful to give up a daughter, he thought, and especially such a daughter as Gertrude. He was touched to the heart; he thought of his own old mother, he thought how gloomy the future had looked to him only a few weeks ago and how sunny it was now; and all these sunny rays shone out from a pair of blue eyes in a sweet, pale, girlish face. He did not know himself how he had happened to speak to her so quickly of his love. He saw again that brilliantly lighted crimson room of yesterday, and the dim twilight in the bow-window room; there she stood in the wonderful light, a mingled moonlight and candle-light. The Christmas tree was lighted in the next room and the voices and laughter of the company floated to his ears. She had turned as he approached her and he had seen tears on her cheeks. But she laughed as she perceived his dismay.

"Ah, it is because Christmas always reminds me of papa. He has been dead seven years yesterday."

One word had led to another and at length they had found their hands clasped together.

"I would gladly have held this little hand fast that time in the church. Would you have been angry, Gertrude?" and she had shaken her head and looked up at him, smiling through her tears, trusting and sweet, this proud young creature—his bride, soon to be his wife!

He started up out of his dream. The carriage stopped at the steps and the house rose dark above him—only behind Aunt Rosa's windows was a light still shining. He went up the steps as if in a dream and entered the garden hall. He looked round as if he had entered the room for the first time, so strange it looked, so changed, so bare and cold. And he thought of the time when someone would be waiting for him here. He could not imagine such happiness.

The door opened softly behind him and as he turned he saw Aunt Rosa appearing like a ghost.

"I have been waiting for you, my dear nephew," she cried out in her shrill voice; "I have found that letter at last, thank Heaven! It is upstairs in your room, and it has taken a weight off my mind, I assure you, Frank." She nodded kindly at him from under her enormous cap. "You are late getting home. I am tired and am going to bed now. Good-night, good-night!"

And she moved lightly like a ghost to the door.

"Auntie!" cried a voice behind her so loud and gay that she turned round in amazement. But then he was beside her and had clasped her in both arms, and before she knew what was happening to her, the shy old maiden lady felt a resounding kiss on her cheek.

"What on earth, Frank Linden—have you gone out of your mind?"

"O, auntie, I can't keep it to myself, I shall choke if I do. So don't be cross. If I had my old mother here, I should kiss the old lady to death for pure bliss. You must congratulate me. Gertrude Baumhagen will be my wife."

Aunt Rosa's half-shocked, half-vexed countenance grew rigid. "Is it possible," she whispered, in amazement, "she will marry into our old house? And the family have consented?"

"A Baumhagen—yes! And she will marry into this old house and the family have consented, Aunt Rosa."

"God's blessing on you! God's richest blessing!" she whispered, but she shook her head and looked at him incredulously. "I shan't sleep a bit to-night," she continued. "I am glad, I rejoice with all my heart, but you might have told me to-morrow. It is done now. Good night, Frank. I am glad indeed; this old house needs a mistress. God grant that she may be a good one." And she pressed his hand as she left him.

He too went to his room. The lamp was burning on the round table and a letter lay beneath it. Ah, true! the long-lost letter! He took it up abstractedly—it was in Wolff's handwriting. He put it down again; what could *he* want? Some business of course. Should he spoil this happy hour with unpleasant, perhaps care-bringing news? No, let the letter wait—till—but he had already taken it up and broken the seal.

It was a long letter and as he read, he bit his lips hard. "Pitiful scoundrel!" he said at length, aloud, "it is well this letter did not reach me sooner, or things would not have happened as they have." And as if shrinking with disgust from the very touch of the paper, he flung it into the nearest drawer of his writing-table.

"Vile wretches, who make the most sacred things a matter of traffic!"

He sat for a long time lost in thought, and a deep furrow marked itself out between his brows. Then he wrote a long letter to his friend, the judge, and gradually his face cleared again—he was telling him about Gertrude.

"BUT HE HAD ALREADY TAKEN IT UP AND BROKEN THE SEAL."

Page 100.

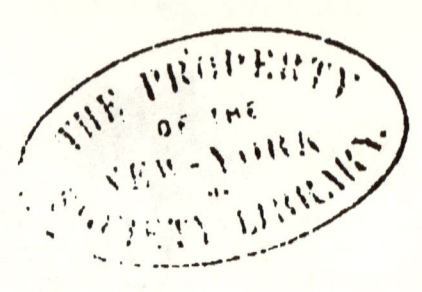

CHAPTER VII.

"GOOD morning, Uncle Henry," said Gertrude, who was sitting at her work-table in the bow-window. She rose as she spoke and went to meet the stout little gentleman as he entered.

"Well, it is lucky that one of you at least is at home," he replied, rubbing his glasses with his red handkerchief, after giving Gertrude's hand a hearty shake. "I wonder if one of the women-kind except you could possibly stay at home for a day. Mrs. Jenny is making calls, Mrs. Ottilie is gone to a coffee party—it is easy to see that a strong hand to hold the reins is wanting here."

Gertrude smiled.

"Uncle, don't scold, but come and sit down," she said. "You come just in time for me ; I had just written a little note to you to ask you to come and see me. I need your advice."

"Oh! but not immediately, child, not immediately! I have just had my dinner," he explained, "and nothing can be more dangerous than hard thinking just after a meal. Ta, ta! There, this is comfortable; now tell me something pleasant, child—about your lover; for instance, how many kisses did he give you yesterday? Honestly now, Gertrude."

He had stretched himself out comfortably in an arm-chair, and his young niece pushed a footstool under his feet and put an afghan over his knees.

"None at all, uncle," she said, gravely; "people do not ask about such things either, you know. Besides I see Frank very seldom," she hesitated. "Mamma goes out so much, and I cannot receive him when she is not at home. And, uncle, it is about that that I wanted to speak to you. Mamma,"—she hesitated again,—"mamma makes me so anxious by all manner of remarks about Linden's circumstances. You know, uncle—"

"And you think she knows all about them?" said the old gentleman. "Oh, of course, ta, ta!"

"Yes, uncle. You see the day before yesterday mamma went out to dine with Jenny, and when she came back she called me into her room, and as soon as I got there I saw that something had happened. Just fancy, uncle, she had been in Niendorf to see, as mamma expressed it, the place where her daughter was going to bury herself. It would be horrible, she declared, to take a young wife to this peasant house; it was not fit for any one to live in; she had felt as if she were in some third-rate farm-house. Linden was sitting in a room—she could touch the ceiling with her hand it was so low, and it was all so poor and common. In short, I could not go there, and if I would not give up my whim of being Mr. Linden's wife, she would have to build a house for me first, for he—he—well, he certainly would not be able to do it, and it would be much more convenient too, to have a snug nest made for him by his mother-in-law. Jenny, who was present at this scene, agreed with her in everything. Oh, uncle, I am so sorry for him, and it is all on my account."

"Did your mother speak to him about building?" asked Uncle Henry.

She drew her hand across her forehead.

"I don't know—I went away without answering. If I had made any reply, it would
have been of no use—we battle with unequal
weapons, or rather I cannot use my weapons,
for she is still my mother."

Her uncle's eyes gazed at her with unmistakable compassion—she was so pale and she
had a weary look about her mouth.

"You poor child! I see they do not make
your engagement time exactly a Paradise to
you," he thought; but he only cleared his
throat and said nothing.

"And what can I do about it?" he asked,
after a pause.

"I am going to tell you that now," said
Gertrude. "You see I have to torment you.
I am not on such terms with Arthur that he
could advise me in this. I want to ask you,
uncle, to speak to Frank—I must know how
great his pecuniary difficulties are, and—"

"Nonsense, child," interrupted the old gentleman, evidently unpleasantly surprised,—
"Why should you drag *me* in? Pecuniary difficulties! What can you do about it? For
the present you have nothing to do with it—
and you will find out about it soon enough."

"You mean because we are not yet man and wife?" she asked.

"Of course!" he nodded.

"O, it is quite the same thing, uncle," she cried, eagerly. "From the moment of our betrothal, I have considered myself as belonging to him entirely, and everything of mine as his. Then why, since I can already dispose of a part of my property as I please, should I not help him out of what may perhaps be a very unpleasant situation?"

"But, my dear child—"

"Let me have my say out, uncle. You know I have ten thousand dollars that came from my grandmother, about which no one has anything to say but myself, and you shall pay over these ten thousand dollars to Linden. I suppose he will have to build—he may need all sorts of things then, and he will be fretted and worried—do this for me, uncle; you see *I* cannot talk to him about such things."

"Indeed, I will not, Miss Gertrude."

"Why?"

"Because he would take it, finally—or he would be angry. Thanks, ever so much."

"But I want him to take it."

He was silent.

"When are you going to be married, child?" he inquired at length.

A rosy flush passed over Gertrude's face—"Mamma has not said anything about it yet. Frank wants it to be in April, and—I do not want to increase his difficulties by my reception."

"Very well, very well, he can wait as long as that," said the old gentleman.

She looked disappointed, but she said nothing.

"I don't want to go against your wishes, little one," he continued, perceiving her sorrowful looks. "I only want to do what is right in matters of business. Now you see if you are bent on following out this plan you will throw away a fine sum of money—in order to make your nest a right comfortable one. *Amantes, amentes*—that is to say in plain English, lovers are mad—and when you wake up to what you have done all your fat is in the fire."

Gertrude said nothing, but she wore a pained expression about her mouth. *He* too spoke so. How often lately had she heard the same thing? Even her pleasure in the single present Linden had made her had been spoiled by similar insulting remarks.

"Oh, don't look so miserable about it, little one," yawned the old gentleman; "what have I said? We men are all egotists with one another I assure you. Why then will you confirm your lover in his egotism and let the roasted larks fly into his mouth beforehand? Keep a tight rein over him, Gertrude, that is the only sensible thing to do; you must not let him be anything more than the Prince Consort—keep the reins of government in your own little fists; confound it, I believe you *can* rule too!"

"Uncle," said the young girl, softly going up to him, "Uncle, you are a hypocrite, you say things that you don't believe yourself. You are all egotists? And I don't know any one in the world who has less claim to the title than you."

"Really, child," he declared, laughing, "I am an egotist of the purest water."

"Indeed? Who gives as much as you to the poor of the city? Who supports the whole family of the poor teacher, with rent, clothes, food and drink? *Who* now, uncle?"

"All selfishness, pure selfishness!" he cried.

"Prove it, uncle, prove it logically."

"Nothing easier. You know the story of how I got a cramp in my leg and dragged myself into the nearest house on the Steinstrasse, and sank down on the first chair I could find. I was just going to dinner; had invited Gustave Seyfried and Augustus Seemann to dine with me—well, you know they have lived in Paris and London. So there I sat in that little low room. The people were at dinner and a dish of thin potato soup stood on the table, that would have been hardly enough for the man alone. Seven children—seven children, mind you, Gertrude,—stood round, and the mother was dealing out their portions. She began with the youngest; the oldest, a lad of fourteen, got the last of the dish. There was not much in it, and I shall never forget the look of those sunken hungry eyes as they rested on that empty bowl. It made me feel so queer all at once. I asked casually, what the man's business was? Teacher of lan-

guage at twelve cents an hour! He could
not get a permanent position on account of
his ill health. Good God, Gertrude! Four
hours a day would give him fifty cents and he
had seven children!

Well, do you know, that day we had oysters
before the soup, and they were rather dear
just then, so I reckoned up that each one of
those smooth little delicacies cost as much as
an hour's lesson, in which the poor man
talked his poor, weak throat hoarse. They
wouldn't go down my throat in spite of their
slipperiness. I couldn't swallow more than
half a dozen and that was disagreeable. At
every course it was the same story, and when
Louis uncorked the champagne, every pop
seemed to go straight to my stomach. I
never ate a more uncomfortable dinner—it
disagreed with me besides, and I had to take
some soda water. 'Confound it!' I said, 'this
thing can't go on,' and—you know, child, that
a good dinner is the purest pleasure in the
world for men of my sort. So there was nothing for me, if I wanted to enjoy my oysters
again, but to comfort myself with the thought
that the seven hungry mouths were also busy

about their dinner. So I sent John to the teacher's wife to ask her how much money she needed a month to feed all seven, with herself and her husband into the bargain, so they would have enough. And, good gracious, it wasn't such an enormous sum, and so I pay her a certain sum every month and I can enjoy my dinner again at the hotel. Now, prove if you can that that isn't pure selfishness."

"Oh, of course, uncle," said the young girl, with brightening eyes, "but I like that sort of selfishness."

"It is all one, Gertrude; I am sending Hannah into retirement now out of selfishness; she is getting so stout that she can't get through the door any more with the coffee tray. And I ask you if I am to keep another servant to open the double doors for her, just for the sake of the old asthmatic woman? That would be fine! So I said to her this morning, 'Hannah, you can go at Easter, and I will continue your wages as a pension.' She was delighted, because she can go to her daughter, now."

"Uncle, I know you very well. I can trust

to you," coaxed Gertrude. "You will speak
to Frank, won't you?"

"Oh, well, yes, yes, only don't blush so.
Now you see you have spoiled my dessert
with all your talking. When does her serene
highness come home?"

"I don't know," replied the young girl.

"To be sure, these coffee-parties are never
to be counted upon. So you two lovers only
see each other on state occasions, like Romeo
and Juliet, or when you have company yourselves?"

Gertrude nodded silently.

"Is it possible!" cried the little gentleman
as he rose to go—"as if the time of an engagement were not the happiest in the world.
Afterwards it is all pure prose, my child.
And they are spoiling this time for you now—
well, you just wait. I must go now to my
card-party. I will look in on your mother
this evening. Good bye; my love to him
when you write."

"Good-bye, uncle. Don't forget that I
shall trust to your selfishness."

When the old gentleman had closed the
door behind him, she sat down to her desk,

took out a letter and began to read it. It was his last letter; it had come this morning and it contained some verses.

How she delighted in these verses in her loneliness! Nothing in the world could separate them! She would indemnify him a thousandfold by her love for all he had to endure now. She tried by a thousand sweet, loving words to make him forget the scorn which her friends scarcely tried to conceal for his boldness and presumption. His manly pride must suffer so greatly under it. More than once the blood had mounted quickly to his forehead, and more than once had he taken leave earlier than he need, as if he could not keep silent and for the sake of peace took refuge in flight.

"I wish I had you in Niendorf now, Gertrude," he had said at the last farewell. "I cannot bear it very patiently to be looked through as if I were only air, by your mother."

And she had nestled closer to him, trembling with agitation.

"Mamma does not mean anything by it, Frank," replied her lips, though her heart knew better. And then he had pressed her passionately to him as he said,

"If I did not love you so much, Gertrude!"

"But it will soon be spring, Frank."

And to-day the verses had come with a bouquet of violets.

She started as she heard Jenny's voice, and immediately after her sister came in, angry and excited.

"I must come to you for a little rest, Gertrude," she said. "Linden is not here? Thank goodness! I can't stand it at home any longer, the baby is so fretful and screams and cries enough to deafen one. The doctor says he must be put to bed, so I have tucked him into his crib. There is always something to upset and fret one."

Gertrude started. Well at any rate he was in good hands with Caroline, she thought.

"Are you going to the masked ball—you and Linden?" asked the young wife.

"No," replied Gertrude, putting away her letter.

"Why not?"

"Why should we go I do not like to dance, as you know, Jenny."

8

" Has Uncle Henry been here ? "

" Yes. Is the baby really ill ? "

" Oh, nonsense ! a little feverish, that is all. We are going to the Dressels this evening. Arthur has sent to Berlin for pictures of costumes, for our quadrille. But you don't care for that. You will bury yourself by and by entirely in Niendorf. The Landrath said to Arthur the other day, 'Your sister-in-law will not be in her proper position; she ought to have married a man in such a position that she would be a leader in society.' You would have been an ornament to any salon and now you are going to the Niendorf cow-stalls."

" And *how* glad I am ! " said Gertrude, her eyes shining.

" Mrs. Fredericks, ma'am," called the pretty maid just then, " won't you please come down ? The baby is so hot and restless."

Jenny nodded, looked hastily at a half-finished piece of embroidery and left the room. When Gertrude followed after a short time she was told that the baby was doing very well and that Mr. and Mrs. Fredericks were dressing for the evening. And so she went upstairs again to her lonely room.

CHAPTER VIII.

A WEEK later the iron-gray horses were bringing the close carriage back from the church-yard at a sharp trot. On the back seat sat Arthur Fredericks with Uncle Henry beside him; opposite was Linden. They wore crape around their hats and a band of crape on the left arm.

The winter had come back once more in full force before taking its final departure. It was snowing, and the great flakes settled down on a little new-made grave within the iron railings of the Baumhagen family burial-place. Jenny's golden-haired darling was dead!

No one in the carriage spoke a word, and when the three gentlemen got out each went his own way after a silent handshake: Uncle Henry to take a glass of cognac, Arthur to his desolate young wife, while Linden went up to Gertrude. He did not find her in the drawing-room; probably she was with her sister.

Presently he heard a slight rustling. He strode across the soft carpet and stood in the open door-way of the room with the bay-window.

"Gertrude!" he cried, in dismay, "for Heaven's sake, what is the matter?"

She was kneeling before her little sofa, her head hidden in her arms, her whole frame convulsed with long, tearless sobs.

"Gertrude!"

He put his arms round her and tried to raise her, when she lifted up her head and stood up.

"Tell me what has happened, Gertrude," he urged; "is it grief for the loss of the little one? I entreat you to be calm—you will make yourself ill."

She had not shed any tears, she only looked deathly pale and her hands, which rested in his, were cold as ice.

"Come," he said, "tell me what it is?" And he drew her towards him.

She clung to him as she had never done before.

"It will be all right again," she whispered, "now I am with you."

"Were you afraid? Has anything happened to you?" he inquired, tenderly.

She nodded.

"Yes," she said, hastily, "a little while ago I chanced to hear a few words mamma was saying to Aunt Pauline—they came up from Jenny's—I suppose they did not think I was here—I don't know. Mamma was still crying very much about the baby and—then she said Jenny must go away—she must have a change—this apathy was so dangerous. You know she has not spoken a word for three days—and—I must accompany her on a long journey—so I—" She stopped and bit her quivering lips.

"So you might forget me if possible?" he inquired, gravely.

He put his hand under her chin and looked into her eyes. She did not reply. but he read the confirmation of his suspicion in her tearful eyes.

"Are they so anxious to be rid of me? Is their dislike so strong, Gertrude? And you?" He felt how she trembled.

"Oh!" she cried with a passion which made Linden start, "Oh, I—do you know there are moments when something seems to take possession of me with the power of a demon—I am swept away by the force of my wrath—I—I do not know what I say and do —I am ashamed now—I ought to have been calm—they cannot separate us, no—they cannot. Now mamma is lying on the sofa in her room and Sophie has gone for the doctor. Ah, Frank, I have borne it all so patiently all these long years—is it so great a sin that my long suppressed feelings should have burst out at last, that my self-control should have given way for once? I was violent—I have always thought I was so calm—those words that I heard seemed to sweep me away like a storm—I don't know what reproaches I may have spoken against my mother. And to-day, just to-day, when they have carried away the only sunbeam that was in this house for me!"

"We will go to your mother, Gertrude, and beg her to pardon us for loving each other so much—come!"

He had said this to comfort her, and because he felt that something must be done. His own desire would have been to take the young girl by the hand and lead her away out of this house.

She freed herself from him and looked at him in amazement. "Ask pardon? And for that?"

"Gertrude, don't misunderstand me." He felt almost embarrassed before her great wondering eyes.

"I meant that we should show your mother calmly and quietly that we cannot give each other up. Say something to her in excuse for your vehemence. Come, I will go with you."

"No, I cannot!" she cried. "I cannot beg forgiveness when I have been so injured in all that I hold most sacred. I cannot!" she reiterated, going past him to the deep window.

He followed her and took her hand; a strange feeling had come over him. Until now he had only seen in her a calm, reasonable woman. But she misunderstood him.

"No!" she cried, "don't ask me, Frank. I will not do it, I cannot, I never could! Not even when I was a child, though she shut me up for hours in a dark room."

"I was not going to urge you," he said;

"only give me your hand, I must know whether this is really you, Gertrude."

She bent down and pressed a kiss on his right hand. "If *you* were not in the world, Frank, if I had to be here all alone!" she whispered warmly.

"But you have all this trouble on my account," he replied, much moved.

She shook her head.

"Only do not misunderstand me," she continued, "and have patience with my faults. You will promise me that, Frank, will you not?" she urged in an anxious tone. "You see I am so perverse when I feel injured; I get as hard as a stone then and everything good seems to die out of me. I could hate those people who thrust their low ideas on me! Frank, you don't know how I have suffered from this already."

They still stood hand in hand. The snow whirled about before the window in the twilight of the short winter day. It was so still here inside, so warm and cosy.

"Frank!" she whispered.

"My Gertrude!"

"You are not angry with me?"

" No, no. We will bear with each other's faults and we will try to improve when we are all alone by our two selves."

" You have no faults," she said, proudly, in a tone of conviction, drawing closer to him.

He was grave.

" Yes, Gertrude, I am very vehement. I sometimes have terrible fits of passion."

" Those are not the worst men," she said, putting her arm round his neck.

" Are you so sure of that ? " he asked, smiling into the lovely face that looked so gentle now in the twilight.

" Yes. My grandmother always said so," she replied.

" The grandmother in the old time ? '

" Yes, dearest. Oh, if you had only known her ! But I should like to see your mother," she added.

" We will go to see her, darling, as soon as we are married. When will that be ? '

" Frank," she said, instead of answering, " don't let us go on a journey at once ; let me know first what it is to have a home where love, trust and mutual understanding dwell together. Let me learn first what *peace* is."

"Yes, my Gertrude. Would to God I could carry you off to the old house to-morrow."

"Gertrude!" called a shrill voice from the next room.

She started.

"Mamma!" she whispered. "Come!" They went together. Mrs. Baumhagen was standing beside her writing-table. Sophie had just brought the lamp, the light of which shone full on the mother's round flushed face, on which rested an unusually decided expression.

"I am glad you are here, Linden," she said to the young man, turning down the leaf of the writing-table and taking her seat before it.

"How much time do you require to put your house in order so that Gertrude could live in it?"

"Not long," he replied. "Some rooms need new carpets, and trifles of that sort—that is all."

"Very well—I shall be satisfied," she replied, coldly. "Then to-morrow you will have the goodness to send your papers in to the clergyman and have the banns published. In three weeks I shall leave for the South with my eldest daughter, and before I go I wish to have this—this affair arranged."

Linden bowed.

" I thank you, madam."

Gertrude stood silent, white to the lips, but she did not look at him. He knew she was suffering tortures for his sake.

" Now I wish to settle some things with my daughter," continued Mrs. Baumhagen, " with regard to her trousseau and the marriage contract."

He turned to go at once, but stopped to kiss his bride's hand and looked at her with imploring eyes. " Be calm," he whispered.

Gertrude laid her hand on her lover's mouth.

" I will have no marriage contract," she said aloud.

" Then your fortune will be common property," was her mother's answer.

"That is what I desire," she replied. "If I can give myself, I will not keep my money from him. That would seem to me beyond measure, foolish."

Mrs. Baumhagen shrugged her shoulders and turned away. The two were standing close together and the bitter words died on her lips.

"Your guardian may talk to you about that," she said. "Will you be so kind, Linden, as to find my brother-in-law? I wish to speak with him."

He kissed Gertrude on the forehead, took his hat and went. Thank Heaven! he should soon be able to shelter her in his own house, this proud young girl who loved him so.

He walked quickly across the square. The fresh air did him good. He felt thoroughly indignant that any one should endeavor to separate them, putting hundreds of miles between them. How easily might a misunderstanding arise, how easily with such a character as hers, whom only the appearance of pettiness would suffice to arouse to scorn, hatred and defiance! How many couples who were deeply attached to each other had been separated in this way before now! He dared not think what would have become of him if it had happened so with them.

"'St!—'St,"—sounded behind him, and as he

turned on the slippery sidewalk he saw Uncle Henry coming down the hotel steps. He had evidently been dining, and his jovial countenance displayed an astonishing mixture of sadness and physical comfort.

" I have had my dinner, Linden," he began, putting his arm through the young man's. " I was very much cast down by this affair of this morning. You don't misunderstand me I hope ? Eh ? I am not one of those who lose their appetites when misfortune comes. I approve of our ancestors who had funeral feasts. I assure you, Linden, that wasn't such a bad idea as we of to-day fancy it. Give all honor to the dead, but the living must have their rights, and to them belong eating and drinking, which keep soul and body together. Ta, ta ! A funeral always upsets me. The poor little fellow ! I was fond of him all the same, you may be sure. I am sure you have not dined yet. Women never eat under such circumstances, every one knows."

" I was just going to look for you," replied Linden. " My future mother-in-law wishes to see you. We—are going to be married in three weeks."

The little man in the fur coat stopped, and looked at Linden as if he did not believe his ears.

" How? What? She has changed her mind very suddenly—did Gertrude improve the opportunity of her softened mood, or—? "

" Gertrude would never do that—no, Mrs. Baumhagen wishes to travel for some time with her eldest daughter, and—"

" Oh, ta, ta! And Gertrude is not to go ? "

" On the contrary—but she would not."

" Aha ! Now it dawns upon me, something has happened. Her serene Highness has been trying—now, I understand—travelling, new scenes, new people—out of sight, out of mind. Ha! ha! she is a born diplomatist. Well, I will come, only let us take the longest way ; the fresh air does me good. I am glad though, heartily glad—in three weeks it is to be then ? "

The gentlemen walked on together in silence through the snow. It was wonderfully quiet in the streets in spite of the traffic of business. Men and carriages seemed to sweep over the white snow. The air was mild, with a slight touch of spring, and Frank Linden

.thought of his home and of the small room next his own, which would not long remain unoccupied.

" How do you do, my dear fellow ! " said a voice beside him, and a little man popped up in front of him, holding his hat high above his bald head—his sharp little face beaming with friendliness. Linden bowed. Uncle Henry carelessly touched the brim of his hat.

" How do you come to know this Wolff ? " he asked, looking after the man, who was winding his way sinuously in and out among the crowd. " He is a fellow who would spoil my appetite if I met him before dinner."

" I am or rather was connected with him by business, through my old uncle—he had money from him on a mortgage on Niendorf," explained Linden.

" From that cravat-manufacturer ? The old man was not very wise."

Linden did not reply. They had just turned into a quiet side-street.

" Does he still hold the mortgage ? " asked Mr. Baumhagen.

" No, my friend's sister has taken it."

" Indeed ! Why did you not come to *me*

about it ?   You could have had some of
Gertrude's money—"

Frank Linden made a gesture of refusal.

"Oh—I promised the child ; she has author-
ized me to put a certain capital at your disposal," explained the old gentleman.

"Thanks," replied Linden, shortly ; "I will
not have money matters mixed up with my
courtship."

"And the new house at Niendorf ? "

"Gertrude knows that she must not expect
a fairy palace.   Moreover we can live very
comfortably there in the old rooms, though
they are low and small.   I have a very pretty
garden-hall, and as for the view from the
windows it would be hard to find another like
it if you travel ever so far."

"Oh, the child is happy enough, but how
about her serene Highness ? " chimed in Mr.
Baumhagen.

"I would far rather have her say, 'My
child has gone to live in a peasant's house,'
than, "*We* had to build first,'" remarked
Linden, drily.

The old gentleman laughed comfortably to
himself.

" Yes, yes, that is just what she would say
—and she wants to go on a journey—it is
astonishing! My dear old mother sought comfort in occupation when my father died—that
was the good old custom—now-a-days people
go on a journey. It would be better for
Jenny, poor thing, if she were to sorrow
deeply here in her home. But no, she must
be dragged away so the whistle of the loco-
motive may drive away her last memory of
her little one's voice. Linden!" The old man
stopped and laid his hand on his shoulder.
"Gertrude is not like that, you may take my
word for it. She would not go away from the
little grave out there—not now. She has her
faults too, but—it is all right with her *here*,"
striking his breast. " Heaven grant she may
be truly happy with you in the old nest. She
has earned it by her sad youth—through her
father."

Frank nodded. He knew it all very well,
just as the old egotist told it to him.

" Well, now we must go," continued Uncle
Henry; "my sister-in-law wants to speak to
me about the wedding, I suppose."

" I think it is about the marriage contract,"

9

said Frank Linden, "and I want to beg you to urge upon Gertrude to yield to her mother's wishes—I shall like it better."

"Hm!" said the old man, clearing his throat. "I yield, thou yieldest, he yields, she —will *not* yield! She is a perverse little monkey—pardon. But it is no use mincing matters. She takes it from her father. He was a splendid man of business, but as soon as his feelings were concerned, away with prudence, wisdom, calculation, and what not. Oh, ta, ta! But here we are."

Mrs. Baumhagen received them very quietly. Gertrude was not with her.

"She is in her room," she said to Linden, as he looked round for her. "She expects you."

He found her in the deep window. There was no lamp in the room, and the light from the fire played on the carpet.

"Gertrude," he said, "how can I thank you!" And he took her hands, which burned in his like fire.

"For what?" she asked.

"For everything, Gertrude! You were

quiet with your mother?" he added, quietly, as she was silent.

"Perfectly so," she replied; "I thought of you. But I am determined not to have a marriage settlement."

"You foolish girl. I might be unfortunate and have bad harvests and things of that sort —then you would suffer too."

She nodded and smiled.

"To be sure, and I would help you with all I possess. And if we have bad harvests and nothing, nothing will succeed, and we have nothing more in the world, then—" she stopped and looked at him with her happy tear-stained eyes—"then we will starve together, won't we, you and I?"

CHAPTER IX.

THE wedding-day came, not as such joyful days usually come. It was as still as death in the house, which was still plunged in the deepest mourning.

The large suite of rooms had been opened and warmed, and over Gertrude's door hung a garland of sober evergreen. The day before the door-bell had had no rest, and one costly · present after another had been handed in. All the magnificence of massive silver, majolica, Persian rugs and other costly things had been spread out on a long table in the bow-window room. A gardener's assistant was still moving softly about in the salon, decorating the improvised altar with orange trees. The fine perfume of *pastilles* lingered in the air and the flame from the open fire was reflected in the glass drops of the chandelier and the smooth *marqueterie* of the floor. Outside, the weather was treacherously mild. It was the first of March.

Mrs. Baumhagen had been crying and groaning all the morning, and between the arrangements for the wedding, she had been giving orders respecting her own journey. The huge trunks stood ready packed in the hall. The next day but one they would start for Heidelberg to see a celebrated doctor.

As for Gertrude's trousseau, her mother had not concerned herself about it—she would attend to it herself. Gertrude's taste was very extraordinary, at the best; if she liked blue Gertrude would be sure to pronounce for red, it had always been so. Ah, this day was a dreadful one to her, and it was only the end of weeks of torture. Since the funeral of the baby, when her daughter had made such a scene, they had been colder than ever to each other. Gertrude's eyes could look so large, so wistful, as if they were always asking, "Why do you disturb my happiness?"

She should be glad when they had fairly started on their journey.

At this time the ladies were all dressing; the wedding was to take place at five o'clock.

The faithful Sophie was helping Gertrude to-day—she would not permit any one to take her place.

Gertrude had put on her wedding-dress, and Sophie was kneeling before her, buttoning the white satin boots.

"Ah, Miss Gertrude," sighed the old woman, "it will be so lonely in the house now. Little Walter dead and you away!"

"But I shall be so happy, Sophie." The soft girlish hand stroked the withered old face which looked up at her so sadly.

"God grant it! God grant it!" murmured the old woman as she rose. "Now comes the veil and the wreath, but I am too clumsy for that, Miss Gertrude—but, ah, here is Mrs. Fredericks."

Jenny entered through the young girl's sitting-room. She wore a dress of deep black transparent crêpe, and a white camellia rested on the soft light braids. She was deathly pale and her eyes were red with weeping.

"I will help you, Gertrude," she said, languidly, beginning to fasten the veil on her sister's brown hair. "Do you remember how you put on my wreath, Gertrude? Ah, if one could only know at such a time what dreadful grief was coming!"

"Jenny," entreated Gertrude, "don't give yourself up to your grief so. When I came down when Walter died, and Arthur was holding you so tenderly in his arms I thought what great comfort you had in each other. That is after all the greatest happiness, when two people can stand by each other, in sorrow and trial."

"Oh," said Jenny, her lip curling disdainfully; "I assure you Arthur is half-comforted already. He can talk of other things, he can eat and drink and go to business, he can even play euchre. Wonderful happiness it is indeed!"

"Ah, Jenny, you cannot expect him to feel the grief that a mother does, he—"

"Oh, you will find it out too," interrupted the young wife. "Men are all selfish."

Gertrude rose suddenly from her chair. She was silent, but her eyes rested reproachfully on her sister as if to say, "Is that the blessing you give me to take with me?"

But her lips said only, "Not all, I know better."

Jenny stood in some embarrassment. " I must go down to Arthur now or he will never be ready at the right time, and then it will be time for me to come up to receive the guests."

The train of her dress swept over the carpet like a dark shadow as she went.

Gertrude sat down for a while in the deep window. The white silk fell in shimmering folds about her beautiful figure, and the grave young face looked out from the misty veil as from a cloud. She folded her hands and looked at her father's picture. "I will take you with me to-night, papa." And her thoughts flew off to the quiet country-house. She did not know it yet. Only once, when she had driven through the village on a picnic, had she seen a sharp-gabled roof and gray walls rising up among the trees. Who would have thought that this would one day be her home !

She felt as if it were heartless in her not to feel the departure from her father's house more. And from her mother ? Ah, her mother ! Papa had loved her, very much at one time. Should she go away without one tear, without one kind motherly word? Gertrude forgot everything in this blissful moment; she remembered only the good, the time when she was a happy child and her mother used to kiss her tenderly. She would not go without a reconciliation.

She rose, gathered up the long train of her wedding-dress and went across the dusky hall to her mother's chamber. She knocked softly and opened the door. .

Mrs. Baumhagen was standing before the tall mirror in a black moiré antique, with black feathers and lace in her still brown hair. Gertrude could see her face in the glass; it was covered thick with powder, which she was just rubbing into her skin with a hare's foot.

Mrs. Baumhagen looked round and gazed at her daughter. She made a lovely bride, far more imposing than Jenny—and all for that Linden! She said nothing, she only sighed heavily and turned back to the glass.

"Mamma," began Gertrude, "I wanted to ask you something."

"In a moment."

Gertrude waited quietly till the last touch

of the powder-puff had been laid on the
temples, then Mrs. Baumhagen took the long
black gloves, seated herself on a lounge at
the foot of her large red-curtained bed, and
began to put them on.

"What do you want, Gertrude?"

"Mamma, what do I want? I wanted to
say good-bye to you." She sat down beside
her mother and took her hand.

Mrs. Baumhagen nodded to her. "Yes, we
sha'n't see each other for some time."

"Mamma, are you still angry with me?"
asked the girl, hesitatingly, her eyes filling
with tears.

"Forgive me, now," she entreated. "I
have been vehement and perverse sometimes,
but—"

"Oh, no matter—don't bring it up now,"
said her mother. "I only hope most heartily
that you may be happy, and may never repent
your obstinacy and perversity."

"Never!" cried Gertrude with perfect conviction.

Mrs. Baumhagen continued to button her
gloves. The room was stifling with the
heavy odors of lavender water and patchouly,

and her heavy silk rustled as she exerted herself to button the somewhat refractory gloves. She made no reply.

"May I ask one more favor, mamma?"

"Certainly."

The girl involuntarily folded her hands in her lap.

"Mamma, show a little kindness to Linden—do try to like him a little—make to-day really a day of honor to him. Oh, mamma," she continued after a pause, "if he is offended to-day it will pierce my heart like a knife—dear mamma—"

The big tears trembled on her lashes.

Once more she asked, "Will you, mamma?"

Mrs. Baumhagen was just ready. She stretched out both her little hands, looked at them inside and out, and said without looking up:

"Kind?—of course—like him? One cannot force one's self to do that, my child. I hardly know him."

"For my sake," Gertrude would have said, but she bethought herself. The days of her childhood had passed, and since then—?"

Mrs. Baumhagen rose.

"It is almost five," she remarked. "Go back to your room. Linden will be here in a moment."

She kissed Gertrude on the forehead, then quickly on the lips.

"Go, my child,—you know I don't like to be upset—God grant you all happiness."

Gertrude went back to her room, chilled to the heart. A tall figure stepped hastily out of the window recess, and a strong arm was around her.

"It is you!" she said, · drawing a long breath, while a rosy flush overspread her face.

———

The little wedding-party were assembled in the salon, the mother, Arthur, Jenny, Aunt Pauline and Uncle Henry. Two young cousins in white tulle made the only points of light amid the gloomy black.

"For Heaven's sake don't wear such long faces!" cried Uncle Henry, who looked as if the wedding had upset him as much as the funeral. "It is dismal enough as it is—"

The door opened and the old clergyman entered. Uncle Henry went to meet him, greeted him loudly, and then disappeared with unusual haste to bring in the bride and bridegroom.

The afternoon sunshine flooded the rich salon, overpowering the light of the candles in the chandelier and the candelabra, and its rays rested on the young couple before the altar.

The voice of the clergyman, sounded mild and clear. They had met for the first time in the house of God, he said ; evidently the Lord had brought them together, and what the Lord had joined together no man should put asunder. He spoke of love which beareth all things, hopeth all things, endureth all things. Gertrude had chosen the text herself.

Then they exchanged rings. They knelt for the blessing, and they rose husband and wife.

Then they went up to their mother. Like Gertrude, Frank Linden saw all things in a different light in this hour. He held out his hand, and though he could find no words, he meant to promise by this hand-shake to guard the life just entrusted to him, as the very apple of his eye, his whole life long.

But Mrs. Baumhagen kissed the young wife daintily on the forehead, laid her fingers as daintily for one moment in his extended hand, and then turned to the clergyman who approached with his congratulations.

The young couple looked at each other, and as he looked into her anxious eyes he pressed her arm closer with his, and she grew calm and almost cheerful.

Uncle Henry had arranged the wedding-dinner, as was to be expected.

The curtains were drawn in the dining-room, which had a northern aspect, the lamps were lighted, and all the family silver shone and sparkled on the table. The old gentleman understood his business. He had had sleepless nights over it lately, it is true, but the *menu* was exquisite. The only pity was that he and Aunt Pauline and Arthur were the only ones who were capable of appreciating it, according to his ideas. The chilling mood still rested on the company, even through Uncle Henry's toasts, not even yielding to the champagne. The old egotist was almost in despair.

When the company adjourned to the drawing-room for coffee, Gertrude went to her room. A quarter of an hour later she came into the hall in her travelling dress. Her husband stood there waiting for her.

From the drawing-room they could hear the murmur of the company—here all was quiet.

She looked round her once more and nodded to the old clock in the corner.

"Good-bye, Sophie," she said, as she went down the staircase on his arm, and the old woman bent over the bannisters in a sudden burst of tears—"Say good-bye to all of them."

Brilliantly lighted windows shone out upon them in Niendorf when Frank lifted her out of the carriage, and led her up the steps. The sky was cloudy, and the fresh spring air was wonderfully soft and odorous.

"Come in !" he cried, opening the brown old house-door.

"Oh, what roses !" she cried with delight.

The balustrade of the staircase, the door-ways, the chains from which the lamps swung were all lavishly adorned with roses, and by the dim light they glowed against the green background as if they were real blossoms.

Kind Aunt Rosa !

Hand in hand they mounted the staircase and walked down the corridor. It was only plastered, but it was quite covered with odorous evergreen. This is our sitting-room, Gertrude, till yours is ready."

She stood on the threshold and looked in with eager eyes. It looked exceedingly cosy and home-like, this low room, pleasantly lighted by the lamp; and a beautiful hunting hound sprang up, whining with joy at sight of his master, whom he had not seen for the whole day. She entered, still holding his hand, in a sort of trembling happiness.

"Oh, what a beautiful dog! And there is your writing-table, and that is the book-case, and what a dear old face that is in the gold frame. Is it your mother, Frank? Yes, I thought she must look like that. And what a pretty tea-table set for two! Oh, dearest!" And the proud spoiled child of luxury lay weeping on his breast.

"Here—it shall remain as it is, Frank—here it is warm and bright; no bitter word can ever be spoken here."

"Don't think of it any more," he whispered, comfortingly. "We have left all evil behind

"THE PROUD SPOILED CHILD OF LUXURY LAY WEEPING IN HIS ARMS."

Page 144.

us. We are owners here, and we will have nothing but peace and love in our household."

"Yes," she said, smiling through her tears, "you are right. What have we to do with the outer world?"

They were standing together in front of his writing-table. A majolica vase stood on it filled with spring flowers.

"What an exquisite scent of violets!" she whispered, drawing in a long breath, and freeing herself from his arms.

A card lay among the flowers. Both hands were extended for it at once.

Heartiest congratulations on your marriage, from

C. WOLFF, Agent.

"How did you happen to know him? *Why* should he send that?" asked her eyes.

But he threw the card carelessly on the table and kissed her on the forehead.

10

CHAPTER X.

Spring is delicious when one is happy. The trees in the Niendorf garden put out their leaves one by one, a green veil hung over the budding forests, and violets were blooming everywhere; Gertrude's whole domain was filled with the scent of the blue children of spring. The voice of the young wife sounded through the old house like the note of a lark, and when Frank returned all sunburned from the fields, a white handkerchief waved from the shining windows upstairs, and when he reached the court it was fluttering in her hand on the topmost step.

"You have come at last, dearest," she would cry then.

And the walks in the woods, the evenings when he read aloud, and then the furnishing the house! How sweet it was to consult together, to make selections, to buy new things and how delighted they both were when they happened to think of the same things!

So the house was furnished by degrees. Workmen and upholsterers did their best. Aunt Rosa's room alone remained untouched, and the master's cosy room, in which they had passed their first happy weeks together.

And now everything was ready, homelike and comfortable without any pretension. The low rooms were not suited to display costly carved furniture, so with excellent taste they had both chosen only the simplest things.

"By-and-by, when we build a new house, Gertrude," he said, and she assented.

"First we will improve the estate, Frank— it is so pleasant in these dear old rooms."

The garden-hall been fitted up as a dining-room. Close by was a drawing-room with dark curtains and soft carpets; on the walls Uncle Henry's wedding present, two large oil paintings—a sunny landscape and a wintry sea-coast. From behind great green palms stood out a noble bust of Hermes. Sofas, low seats and arm-chairs everywhere, and wherever there was the smallest space it was filled up with a vase of fresh flowers.

Upstairs, next to the master's room, was that of the young wife, where her father's picture now stood behind the work-table, by the window.

The door between the two rooms stood open, and bright striped Turkish curtains drawn back, permitted Gertrude from her place by the window, to see the writing-table at which he was working. And from the window might be seen the wooded mountains beyond the green garden, and farther away still the distant Brocken, half-hidden in the clouds.

The young wife had cleared out all the cupboards ; in the kitchen the last new tin had been hung up on the hooks, and shone and sparkled in the bright sunshine as if it were pure silver. In the store-room jars and pots were all full and in order, as she turned the key with a happy smile, and put it into the spick-and-span new key-basket on her arm.

"Come, Frank," she said, after he had been admiring all this splendor, "now we will go through all the rooms again."

"There are not many of them, Gertrude," he laughed.

"Enough for us, Frank ; we do not need any more."

And they went through the garden hall, and admired the stately buffet and the hanging-lamp of polished brass, which swung over the great dining-table. They went into the drawing-room, and admired the pictures again which the sun lighted up so beautifully, and then they stopped, looked in each other's eyes and kissed each other.

"It is all just as I like it, Frank," said she, "plain and suitable, but nothing sham, no imitations. I hate pretence—everything ought to be genuine, as real and true as my love and your heart, you dear, good fellow.—Now everything is perfect in the house," she continued, picking up a thread from the carpet. "No one would recognize it; it is the most charming little house for miles around. And it did not cost nearly as much as Jenny's trousseau and wedding-journey."

They were standing in the open hall door, and the young man looked with brightening eyes across the garden to the outbuildings which had exchanged their leaky roofs for new shining blue slates.

"You are right, Gertrude, it is a pretty sight; we will sit here often. And to-morrow they will begin to build the new barns. They must be ready when we harvest the first rye."

"Frank," she asked, mischievously, "do you still think as you did a week after our wedding when we spoke about this for the first time, and you were really childish and absolutely *would* not take anything of that which is yours by every right human and divine? And you would have let the cows be rained on in their stalls and the farm-servants in their beds."

"No, Gertrude, not now," he replied.

"And why, you Iron-will?"

"Because we love each other, love each other unspeakably."

"The adjective is not necessary," corrected she.

"Don't you believe that one may love unspeakably?" asked he with a smile.

"It sounds like a figure of speech."

He laughed aloud, and drew her out on the veranda.

"Our home," he said; "come, let us go

through the garden and a little way into the wood."

The next day Gertrude opened the windows of the guest-chamber, and made everything there bright and fresh. The table in the dining-room was gayly decked, and Frank drove to the city in the new carriage to bring the judge from the station.

Gertrude was glad of the opportunity of seeing him, Frank had told her so much about his old friend. She had laughed heartily over his droll descriptions of his friend's peculiarities, how in company when he tried to pay a compliment he invariably managed to make it a back-handed one, to his own infinite astonment.

She would take especial pains with her dress for this "jewel" of a man, as Frank called him. She put a rosette of lace in her hair, Frank liked that so much, it looked so matronly, almost like a little cap. When she went up to the toilet-table with this graceful emblem of her youthful dignity, to look at herself in the glass, she saw there a bouquet of lilies of the valley with a paper wound round their stems.

"From him, from Frank," she whispered, growing crimson with delight.

He had said good-bye to her with such a merry smile. She hastily unwound the paper from the flowers and read it.

They were verses turning on the expression he had made use of the day before,—"loving unspeakably," and justifying himself for using it by pointing out that for long after he had seen and loved her he knew not how to call her, where she dwelt, nor who she was, and so he might literally be said to have loved her "unspeakably."

"That is how he proves himself in the right," she murmured with blissful looks, pressing the paper to her lips. "And he is right, indeed, he does love me 'unspeakably.' Ah, I am a very happy woman!"

And she put the lilies of the valley in her dress, the verses in her pocket, took the key-basket and went to the dining-room once more on a tour of inspection round the table, and then as she had nothing to do for the moment, she knocked at Aunt Rosa's door, which was only separated from the dining-room by a small entry.

The old lady was sitting at the window making roses. There was to be a wedding in the village at Whitsuntide. A small man was sitting opposite her, who greeted the entrance of the young wife with a low bow.

"Beg a thousand pardons, madam,—I wanted to speak to your husband—I heard he had gone out and the lady here permitted me to wait for him."

"What does he say, Mrs. Linden?" inquired the old lady, shaking hands, "I did not permit him to do any such thing. He came in himself—and here he is."

"My name is Wolff, madam," said the agent by way of introduction.

"Must you speak to my husband to-day? It will not be convenient, for we have company to dinner. Can't I arrange it?" inquired Gertrude.

"O, no—no—" said he, very decidedly, bowing as he spoke. "I must speak to Mr. Linden himself, but I can come again, there is no hurry, I used to come here every day. Good morning, ladies."

"What could he want, auntie?" inquired the young wife after he had gone.

"Well, I can tell you what he wanted of *me*—he wanted to *question* me. He would have liked to look through the key-hole to find out how it looked in your house. But sit down, my dear."

These two understood each other perfectly. Sometimes the old lady drank coffee with Gertrude and then she had many questions to answer. In this way it had come out quite by chance that she had been a schoolmate of Gertrude's grandmother.

Sometimes they went to walk together and Gertrude learned to know the village people, found out who the poor ones were and a little of the history of the place. Aunt Rosa's pictures were rather roughly drawn, she did not like every one, but Linden was her idol next to a young niece of hers.

" He is so nice," she used to say, " he is so courteous to the old as well as the young."

And Gertrude returned the compliment by declaring she could not imagine the house without Aunt Rosa.

To-day, the young mistress of the house could not stay long quietly in the rose-room. It was strange, but she felt anxious about her husband. If only he had had no accident with the new horses, she thought, as she went out on the veranda.

The blooming garden lay quiet and still before her in the mid-day sunshine. Suddenly a shadow came over her face—there, under the chestnut-trees, where the sunbeams broke through the leaves in golden flecks. There was no doubt of it—it was he, the man in Aunt Rosa's room. How happened he to penetrate into the garden? Where had she heard his name before? She started as if she had touched something unpleasant. "Wolff," —it was the name on the card that came with the flowers on her wedding eve. Yes, to be sure. But she had *seen* the man, too, somewhere before—where was it? Perhaps in the factory with Arthur, very likely.

She raised her head and her eyes began to sparkle. There was the carriage just turning in at the gate. *He* was driving and on the front seat beside the expected guest sat Uncle Henry, waving his red handkerchief.

The gentlemen were all in the best of humor—it was a lively meeting.

" It looks something like here now, Frank,"

said the little judge, clapping Linden on the shoulder and shaking hands with his wife. He was so pleased that he even inquired for Aunt Rosa.

" Do you know, child," said Uncle Henry by way of excuse for his presence, " I should not be here so soon again, but the landlord of the hotel died this morning—and I couldn't eat there, it was out of the question. You have some asparagus ? "

" I shall not tell any tales out of school, uncle."

She put her arm in that of the old gentleman and went up the steps with her guests. At the top she turned her head and then walked quickly to the balustrade of the veranda.

There stood Wolff bowing before her husband, his hat in his hand, his face covered with smiles.

" O, ta, ta ! " said Uncle Henry.

" How comes he here, Gertrude ? "

The judge looked out from under his blue spectacles with earnest attention at the two men. Just then Linden waved his hand shortly and they strode along the way which led to the court and the outer gate, Wolff still speaking eagerly.

Gertrude bent far over the iron railing. It seemed to her that Frank was vexed. Now they stood still. Frank opened the gate and pointed outward with an unmistakable and very energetic gesture.

Mr. Wolff hesitated, he began to speak again—again the mute gesture still more energetic, and the little man disappeared like a flash. The gate fell clanging in the lock and Frank came back, but slowly as if he must recover himself first and deeply flushed as if from intense anger.

Gertrude went to meet him, but said nothing. She would not ask him for explanations before their guests. She very stealthily pressed his hand and spoke cheerfully of her pleasure in her guests.

" Charming ! " he said, absently, " but Gertrude, pray entertain Uncle Henry—Richard —come with me a moment—I must—I will show you your room." And the two friends left the room together.

" Do you know that you are going to have some more visitors this afternoon ? " asked the old gentleman, settling himself comfortably in a chair. " Your mother and the Fredericks,—they came back yesterday morning. Jenny looks blooming as a rose, and, thank Heaven! Arthur has got his milk-face burned a little with the sun."

" Yes," replied Gertrude, " he was with them at the Italian lakes for a month." And then as if she had only just taken in his whole meaning,—" How glad I am that mamma is coming out here at once! Ah, uncle, if she would only get reconciled to Frank ! "

" Eh, what ? Gertrude, don't distress yourself, it will all come right. Besides he is not a man to put up with much nonsense ! "

" What could this Wolff have wanted with him ? "

" Hm ! what are they about in Heaven's name ? " asked her uncle, impatiently.

" Are you hungry ? " she asked, absently.

" Hungry ? How can you use such common expressions ? A dish of pork and beans would suffice for hunger. I have an appetite, my child. O, ta, ta, the asparagus will be spoiled if those two stay so long in their room."

It was a very cosy group that Mrs. Baumhagen's eyes rested on as she, with Jenny and Arthur, mounted the veranda steps.

They were sitting over their dessert, and Uncle Henry, with his napkin in his buttonhole, his champagne-glass in his hand, shouted out a stentorious "welcome!" while the young host and hostess hurried down the steps, Gertrude with crimson cheeks. She was so proud, so happy.

Mrs. Baumhagen looked at her daughter in amazement. The pale, quiet girl had become as blooming as a rose. "It is the honeymoon still," she said to herself, and her eyes never ceased to follow her youngest child during the whole time of her stay.

The coffee-table was set out under the chestnuts. It was a beautiful spot. The eye glanced over the green lawn, past the magnificent trees to the quaint old dwelling-house with its high gables and its ivy-grown walls. The doors of the garden-hall stood open, and from the flagstaff fluttered gayly a black-and-white flag.

"An idyll like a picture by Voss," laughed the little judge.

The young host gallantly escorted his mother-in-law through the garden. Every cloud had vanished from his brow, he was cheerful and agreeable.

"But very sure of himself," Jenny remarked, later, to her mother. "He feels himself quite the host and master of the house."

The uncomfortable feeling which he had always had in his mother-in-law's presence, had disappeared. To her amazement he permitted himself once or twice quite calmly to contradict her. Arthur had never dared to do that. And Gertrude, how ridiculous! while she presided over the coffee in her calm way, her eyes were continually turning to him as soon as he spoke. "As you like, Frank,"— "What do you think, Frank?" etc. And when her mother hoped Gertrude would not fail to call on her Aunt Pauline on her birthday, the next day, she asked appealingly, "Can I, Frank? Can I have the carriage?"

"Certainly, Gertrude," was the reply.

Then Mrs. Baumhagen put down her dainty coffee cup and leaned back in her garden chair. The child was not in her right mind!

that was too much. But Arthur Fredericks applauded loudly.

"Gertrude," he called out across the table, "talk to this—" he seized the hand of his wife who angrily tried to draw it away. "What does Katherine say as an amiable wife to her sister? Words that sound as sweet to us as a message from a better world."

"To be sure!" laughed Gertrude, not in the least offended by the ironical tone.

"Thy husband is thy lord, thy life, thy keeper,
Thy head, thy sovereign; one that cares for thee
And for thy maintenance; commits his body
To painful labor, both by sea and land;
To watch the night in storms, the day in cold
While thou liest warm at home secure and safe;
And craves no other tribute at thy hands
But love, fair looks and true obedience,—
Too little payment for so great a debt."

"You see, Arthur, I have my Shakespeare at my tongue's end."

Mrs. Baumhagen suddenly broke up the coffee party. She seemed heated, for she was fanning herself with her handkerchief.

"Gertrude, you must show us the house,"
11

she exclaimed. " Come, Jenny, we will leave
the gentlemen to their cigars."

" Gladly, mamma," said the young girl,
easily.

She led her mother and sister through the
kitchen and cellar, through the chambers, and
through the whole house. In the dining-room
a pretty young woman in a spotless white
apron was engaged in clearing off the table.
Gertrude gave her some orders in a low tone
as she passed.

" That is Johanna, whose husband was
killed," said Jenny.

" Yes," replied her sister, " I have engaged
her as housekeeper. She is very capable,
and I like to have a familiar face about me."

" With the child?" asked the mother,
scornfully.

" Of course," replied the young wife.
" She lives in the other wing. It is a pleasure to see how the little fellow improves in
the country air."

" Who lives in this wing?" inquired Jenny.

" Aunt Rosa."

" Good gracious! A sort of mother-in-
law?" cried her sister in consternation.

Gertrude shook her head. " No, she is quite inoffensive, she belongs to the inventory —so to speak. But I would like Frank to have his mother here, the old lady is so alone and she is not very well."

Jenny laughed aloud, but Mrs. Baumhagen rustled so angrily into the next room that all the ribbons on her rather youthful toilette fluttered and waved in the air.

"Gertrude!" cried Jenny, " you will not be so senseless ! "

The young wife made no reply. She opened a wardrobe door in the corridor and said,

" This is the linen, Jenny; we need so much in the country. That is the chest for the finest linen and for the china, and this is my room. This way, mamma."

" It might have been a little less simple," remarked her mother, who had recovered herself, though the flush of excitement still rested on her full cheeks.

" I did not wish to be so very unlike Frank, who kept his old furniture ; besides we are only in moderate circumstances, you know, mamma, and we are only just beginning."

Her mother cleared her throat and sat down in one of the small arm-chairs. Jenny wandered about the room, looking at the pictures and ornaments, slightly humming to herself as she did so. Gertrude stood thoughtfully beside her mother and felt her heart grow cold as ice. It was the old feeling of estrangement which always thrust itself between her and her mother and sister—they had nothing in common. She grieved over it as she had always done, but she no longer felt the bitter pain of former days. Slowly her hand sought the pocket of her dress, and touched lightly a rustling paper—"Thou art unspeakably beloved." Ah, that was compensation enough for anything, and she lifted her head with a happy smile.

"But you have not told me anything about your delightful journey yet, and your letters were so very short."

"O, yes," said Jenny, yawning as she took up a terra cotta figure and gazed at it on all sides, "it was perfectly delightful in Nice. Now that I am back again, I begin to feel what a provincial little circle it is that we vegetate in here."

"We will go again, next year, Providence permitting," added Mrs. Baumhagen. "Only I must beg to be excused from Arthur's company. He was really just as childish as your father used to be in his time. Jenny must not do this and Jenny should not do that, mustn't go here and mustn't stand there, in short he was a perfect torment, as if we women did not know ourselves what it is proper to do."

Jenny seated herself too.

"Never mind, mamma, he is still suffering for his folly. I have not allowed him to forget the scene he made for us at Monte Carlo yet."

"O yes, Heaven knows you are a very happy couple," exclaimed her mother.

"But I think it is time for us to be going home," she continued, taking her costly watch from her belt. "We will go and get your husband. Come."

The three ladies went back to the garden to the table where the gentlemen were comfortably chatting over their cigars. Frank was in earnest conversation with Aunt Rosa, who in her best array, sat enthroned in the

seat Mrs. Baumhagen had left only a short
time before. Gertrude hastened to introduce
her mother and sister to the old lady. There
was no help for it—they were obliged to sit
down again for a short time out of politeness.
Mrs. Baumhagen, with a bored look, Jenny
with scarcely concealed amusement at the
wonderful little old lady.

"Gertrude," began Frank, "Aunt Rosa
came to tell us that she expects company."

"I hope it won't put you out," said the old
lady, turning to Gertrude. "My niece always
visits me every year at this time. You have
heard me say that the child is passionately
fond of the woods and mountains and she
cheers me up a little."

"Is it that pretty little girl you have told
us about so often, Aunt Rosa?" asked Gertrude, kindly; and as the former nodded, she
continued,

"Oh, she will be heartily welcome, won't
she, Frank? When is she coming, and what
is her name?"

"I expect her in a day or two, and her
name is Adelaide Strom," replied Aunt Rosa.
"I always call her Addie."

"GERTRUDE HASTENED TO INTRODUCE HER MOTHER AND SISTER TO THE OLD LADY."

Page 166.

Then she began to explain the relationship which had the result of making all the company dizzy.

"My mother's sister married a Strom, and her step-son is the cousin of Adelaide's grand-father—"

Here Mrs. Baumhagen rose with a great rustling. "I must go home," she said, interrupting the explanation. "It is high time we were gone."

Jenny, who was standing behind her husband's chair, laid her hand on his shoulder.

"Please order the carriage."

"Why, what do you mean, child?" said he in a tone of vexation. "We have only just come!"

"But mamma wishes it."

"Mamma? But why?" he asked, shortly. "We are having a delightful talk."

"Won't you stay till evening, Mrs. Baumhagen?" asked Frank, courteously.

"My head aches a little," was the reply.

Arthur ran his hand despairingly through his hair. This "headache" was the weapon with which every reasonable argument was overthrown.

"Very well, then, do you go," he muttered, grimly. "I will come home with Uncle Henry."

"Yes, to be sure, my dear fellow," cried the old gentleman, much pleased. "I shall be very glad of your company; we will try the Moselle, eh, Frank?"

"Uncle Henry filled up the cellar for our wedding-present," explained the young host as he rose to order the carriage.

"And so richly," added Gertrude.

"Oh, ta, ta!"

The old gentleman had risen and was helping his sister-in-law on with her cloak, with somewhat asthmatic politeness.

"It was pure selfishness, Ottilie. Only that a man might get a drop fit to drink when one arrived here, weary and thirsty."

"Gertrude," whispered Jenny, taking her sister a little aside, "how can you be so foolish as to allow a young girl to be brought into the house? I tell you it is really dreadful; they are always in the way, they *always* want to be admired, they are always wanting to help and never fail to pay most touching attentions to the host. It is really inconsider-

ate of the old lady to impose her on you.
Invent some excuse for keeping her away.
I speak from experience, my love. Arthur
invited a cousin once, you remember. I
nearly died of vexation."

Gertrude laughed.

"Ah, Jenny," she said, shaking her head.
The she hastened after her mother who was
already seated in the carriage.

"Come again soon," she said cordially,
when Jenny had taken her seat also.

"I shall expect a visit from you next," was
the reply. "You must be making a few calls
in town some time."

"We haven't thought about it yet," cried
Gertrude, gayly.

"Pray do see that Arthur gets home before
the small hours. Uncle Henry never knows
when to go," cried Jenny in a tone of vexation.

And the carriage rolled away.

CHAPTER XI.

It was late before Uncle Henry and Arthur set out for home and late when the little judge went to his room. They had all three sat for a good while in Frank's study, talking of past and present times.

"We shall be very gay," said Frank, "when Aunt Rosa's niece comes. You will not be so much alone then, Gertrude, when I am away in the fields."

"I am never lonely," she replied, quietly. "I have never had a girl-friend, and now it seems superfluous to me." And she looked at him with her grave deep eyes.

"Madam," inquired the judge, putting the end of his cigar in a meerschaum mouthpiece, "has he written poetry to you too?" And he pointed to Frank with a sly laugh.

Gertrude flushed.

"Of course," she replied.

"Ah, he can't help writing verses," said the

170

little man, teasingly, clapping his friend on
the shoulder.

" I tell you, Mrs. Linden, sometimes it seizes
upon him like a perfect fever; and the things
that a fellow like that finds to write about!
Poets really are born liars. At the moment
when the sweet verses flow out on the paper,
they actually believe every word they write—it
is really touching ! "

" Spare me, Richard, I beg of you," laughed
the young host, half angrily.

" Isn't it true? " asked the judge. " Only
think of your celebrated poem on the gypsy
girl. I was there when you saw the brown
maiden on the Römerberg, and in the evening
it was already written down in your note-book
that she wandered through the streets with
winged feet, with straying hair, and shy black
eyes in which a longing for the moorland lay
and for the wind which through the reed-grass
sweeps—and so on. Ha, ha ! And she really
came from the Jew's quarter and went begging
from house to house for old rags."

They all three laughed, Gertrude the most
heartily ; then she became suddenly grave.

" You are a malicious fellow," declared

Frank, rising to light a candle. "It is late, Richard, and we are early risers here."

As the friends bade each other good-night at the door of the guest-chamber, the judge said,

"Well, Frank, I congratulate you. You have won a prize—such a dear, sensible little woman!

"As for the *other*—my dear fellow, what did I tell you about that man? Well, good-night! That Uncle Henry is a good old soul, too,—now take yourself off."

Gertrude was standing by the open window in her room, looking out into the night. The lamplight from the next room shone in faintly. Dark clouds were gathering, far away over the mountains there were flashes of lightning and in the garden a chorus of nightingales was singing.

"Gertrude," said a voice behind her.

"Frank," she replied, leaning her head on his shoulder.

"Hush! Listen! It is so lovely to-night."

They stood thus for awhile in silence. This afternoon's conversation was still linger-

ing in Linden's mind. Uncle Henry could
not understand why he should not cut his
timber from his own woods. But the Niendorf woods had been greatly thinned out and
no new plantations made.

"Tell me, Gertrude," he began, suddenly,
" where is your villa ' Waldruhe ? ' "

His young wife started as if a snake had
stung her. " Our—my villa ? " she gasped,
" how did you know—who told you about the
villa ? "

He was silent. " I cannot remember who,"
he said after a pause, " but some one must
have told me that there is a little wood belonging to it. But, Gertrude, what is the matter ? "
he inquired. " You are trembling ! "

"Ah, Frank, who told you about *that ?* " she
reiterated, " and *what ?* "

Her voice had so sad a ring in it that he
perceived at once that he had hurt her.

"Gertrude, have I hurt you? I beg your
pardon a thousand times ; I was only thinking
of cheaper timber which I might have cut
there this winter."

" Timber ? There ? It is only a park.
Ah, Frank—"

"But what is it pray?" he asked with a little impatience. "I cannot possibly know—"

"No, you cannot know," she assented. "It was only the shock—I ought to have told you long ago, only it is so frightfully hard for me to speak of it. You ought to know about it too, but—tell me who told you about it?"

"But when I assure you, my child, that I cannot remember."

"Frank," said his young wife, in a low, hesitating tone, "out there—in 'Waldruhe,' my poor father died—"

"My little wife!" he said, comfortingly.

"It was there—he—he killed himself." Her voice was scarcely audible.

He bent down over her, greatly shocked. "My poor child, I did not know that, or I would not have spoken of it."

"And I found him, Frank. He built 'Waldruhe' when I was but a child, and he used to go and stay there for weeks together. It is so hard to talk of it—he was not happy, Frank. Ah, we will not dwell on it. Mamma did not understand him, and it was the day after Christmas and I knew they had

"HE was up stairs—yes—but he was dead."

Page 175.

had a dispute ; that is not the right word for
it either, for papa never contradicted her, and
he bore so patiently all her crying and complaining. After awhile I heard the carriage
drive away. It was in the morning—and I had
such a strange feeling of anxiety and dread
and after dinner I put on my hat and cloak
and ran out of the Bergedorf gate along the
high road, on and on till I came to 'Waldruhe.' I was surprised to see that the blinds
were shut in his room, but I saw the fresh
wheel-tracks in front of the house. The gardener's wife, who lives in a little cottage on
the place, said he was upstairs. He *was* upstairs—yes—but he was dead !"

She stood close beside him, encircled by
his arm, as she told her story. He could feel
how she trembled and how cold her hands
were.

"Don't speak of it any more, my darling,"
he entreated, "you will make yourself ill."

"Yes, I was ill, Frank, for a whole year,"
she said. "It was a fearful time ; I could not
forgive my mother. From that moment the
gulf arose which parts us to-day, and nothing
can bridge it over. I was so horribly lonely,

Frank, before I found you. But the villa?—
Yes, it belongs to me ; papa destined it for me
when he built it. I have had some very
pleasant days with him there, but now the very
thought of it is dreadful to me. It is empty
and deserted. I have never been there since.
It is so horrible to find a person whom one
has so honored and loved—to find him so—"

" Forgive me, Gertrude," he said, gently.

"You could not know, Frank. No one
knows it but ourselves." And as if to turn
his thoughts to something else she continued
hurriedly, " Thank you so much, love, for that
lovely poem, 'Thou art unspeakably beloved.' "

And she stroked his hand and pressed it to
her lips.

" My poor little Gertrude ! "

They stood thus together for awhile
wrapped about with the sweet atmosphere of
spring.

" A thunder-shower is coming up," he said
at length ; and she freed herself from his arms
and left the room. Frank could hear her going softly about the corridor here and there,
shutting the doors and windows, and jingling

her keys. She was looking to see if everything was in order for the night.

He put his hand to his forehead and tried
to recall who had spoken to him of the villa.
He passed on into his lighted room as if he
could think better there. After awhile the
young wife came back, with her key-basket
on her arm. The sweet face was lifted up to
him.

"Frank," said she, "what did the agent
want of you to-day?"

He stared at her as if a flash of lightning
had struck him.

"That is it! that is it!" And he struck
his forehead as if something he had been seek-
ing for in vain had suddenly occurred to him.

"What did he want? Oh, nothing, Gertrude, nothing of any consequence."

She looked at him in surprise, but she said
nothing. It was not her way to ask a second
time when she got no answer. It really was
of no consequence.

12

CHAPTER XII.

It had rained heavily in the night, with thunder and lightning, but nature seemed to have no mind to-day to carry out her coquettish love of contrasts; she did not laugh, as usual, with redoubled gayety in blue sky and golden sunshine on forest and field: gloomily she spread a gray curtain over the landscape, so uniformly gray that the sun could not find the smallest cleft through which to send down a friendly greeting, and it rained unceasingly, a perfect country rain.

Frank came back from the fields rejoicing over the weather, and Gertrude waved her handkerchief to him out of the window as she did every morning.

"All the flowers are ruined, Frank," she cried down to him, "what a pity!"

He came up in high good humor. "No money could pay for this rain, darling," he said; "I am a real farmer now, my mood varies according to the weather."

"And mine too!" remarked his wife. "Such a gray day makes me melancholy."

He went towards her as she sat at her writing-table turning over books and papers.

"Just look, Frank," as she held out to him a packet daintily tied up with blue ribbons; "these are all verses of yours, arranged according to order. When we have our silver wedding I shall have them printed and bound. These on cream-colored paper were written during our engagement, and these different scraps, white and blue and gray, were written since our marriage, when you take anything that comes, thinking I suppose that it is good enough for *Mrs.* Gertrude."

She looked up at him with a smile. He bent down over her.

"And now I shall buy a very special kind of paper for my next verses, Gertrude."

"Why?"

"Bright, like the little bundles the storks carry under their wings. And I shall write on it—"

She grew crimson. "A cradle-song," she finished softly.

He nodded and put her hand to his lips. But she threw both arms round his neck. "Then it would be sweet and home-like, Frank. Then we should love each other better than ever—if that were possible."

"Here, little wife, I wrote this for you to-day in the field in the rain." He took out his note-book from his pocket and put it in her hand.

"I will just go and see what the judge is about, the rascal," he called back from the door.

And she sat still and read, her face as grave and earnest as if she were reading in the Bible.

She was startled from her reading by the snapping of a whip before the window. She looked out quickly—there stood the Baum-hagen carriage; the coachman in his white rubber coat and the cover drawn over his hat, the iron-gray horses black with the drenching rain. She opened the window to see if any one got out. Johanna came out and the coachman gave her a letter with which she ran quickly back into the house.

Gertrude was startled. An accident at home? She flew to the door.

"A letter, ma'am."

She hastily tore it open.

"Come at once—I must speak to you without delay.

"YOUR MOTHER."

Such were the oracularly brief contents of the note.

"Bring me my things, Johanna, and tell my husband."

"Frank," she cried, as he entered, hurriedly, "something must have happened."

"Don't be alarmed," he besought her, though unable quite to conceal his own uneasiness.

"Yes, yes. Oh, if I only knew what it was! I feel so anxious."

He took her things from the servant and put the cloak round Gertrude's shoulders.

"I hope it has nothing to do with Arthur and Jenny. They were very strange to each other, yesterday."

Gertrude looked at him and shook her head. "No, no, they were always like that."

"Then I am surprised that he did not run away long ago," he said, drily.

"Or she," retorted Gertrude tying her bonnet.

"I could not stand such everlasting complaints, Gertrude," said he, buttoning her left glove.

"Nor I, Frank. Good-bye. You must make my excuses at dinner. God grant it is nothing very bad."

She looked round the room once more, then went quickly up to her work-table and thrust the note-book into her pocket.

When a few minutes later the landau passed out of the great iron gate she put her head out of the window. He stood on the steps looking after her. As she turned he took off his hat and waved it.

How handsome he was, how stately and how good!

She leaned back on the cushions. She felt a vague alarm—it was the first time she had left the house without him. Strange thoughts came over her—how dreadful it would be if

she should not find him again, or even—if
she should lose him utterly. Could she go on
living then? Live—yes—but how?

It would be frightful to be a widow! Still
more frightful if they were to part—one here,
the other there, hating each other, or indiffer-
ent!

Could Arthur and Jenny, really—? Oh,
God in Heaven preserve us from such woe!

She looked out of the window. The coachman was driving at a dizzy pace. There lay
the city before her in the mist. Again her
thoughts wandered, faster than the horses
went. She took the note-book out of her
pocket to read the verses, but the letters
danced before her eyes, and she put it away
again.

In the attic at home stood the old cradle in
which her father had been rocked, and Jenny,
and she herself. The grandmother in the
narrow street had had it as part of her outfit.
She would get it out for herself if God should
ever fulfil her wish. Jenny's darling had lain
in another bed, the clumsy old cradle did not
seem suitable in the elegant chamber of the
young mother, but in the modest room at

Niendorf, where the vines crept about the windows and the big old stove looked so cosy and comfortable, it would be quite in place, just between the stove and the wardrobe in a cosy corner by itself. She smiled like a happy child. She could not believe that her life could be so beautiful, so rich.

The carriage was now rattling through the city gate; she would be at home in a minute now, and her heart began to beat loudly. If she only knew what it was.

The porter opened the carriage door and she got out and ran up the stairs to Jenny's apartment. The entrance door of her mother's apartment stood open. No one was to be seen and she entered the hall. How dear and familiar everything looked! Even the tall clock lifted up its voice, and struck the quarter before two. She took off her cloak and went to her mother's room. Here, too, the door was ajar. Just as she was going to enter she suddenly drew back her hand.

"And I tell you, Ottilie, it will be the worst act of your life, if you fling all this in the child's face without the slightest preparation.

Whether it is true or false why should you destroy her young happiness? There are other ways and means."

It was Uncle Henry. He spoke in a tone of the deepest vexation.

"Shall she hear it from strangers?" cried the voice of her weeping mother; "the whole town is ringing with it, and is she to go about as if she were blind and deaf?"

"I am trembling all over," Gertrude now heard Jenny say; "it is outrageous, we are made forever ridiculous. It was only last evening that I said to Mrs. S——, 'You can't imagine what an idyllic Arcadian happiness has its dwelling out there in Niendorf.'"

"Confound your logic! I tell you—" cried the little man angrily. But he stopped suddenly, for there on the threshold stood Gertrude Linden.

"Are you talking of us?" she asked, her terrified eyes wandering over the group and resting at length on her mother, who at sight of her had sunk back weeping in her chair.

"Yes, child."

The old man hastened towards her and tried to draw her away.

" It's a thoughtless whim of your mother to send for you here ; nothing at all has happened ; really, it is only some stupid gossip, a misunderstanding perfectly absurd. Come across to the other room and I will explain it all."

" No, no, uncle, I must know it, must know it all."

She withdrew her hand from his and went up to her mother.

" Here I am, mamma; now tell me everything, but quickly, I entreat you."

She looked down on the weeping woman with a face that was deathly pale, standing motionless before her in her light summer costume. Only the strings of her bonnet, which were tied on the side in a simple bow, rose and fell quickly, and bore witness to her great agitation.

" I can't tell her," sobbed Mrs. Baumhagen, " you tell her, Jenny."

Gertrude turned to her sister at once. She cast down her eyes and wound the black velvet ribbon of her morning-dress nervously round her finger.

" Your husband is in a very unpleasant situation," she began in a low tone.

"In what respect?" asked Gertrude.

"It is a disagreeable affair, but nothing to make such solemn faces over," burst out the old gentleman, who was standing at the window.

"He had—" Jenny hesitated again, "a conversation with Wolff yesterday."

"I know it," replied Gertrude.

"Wolff had a claim on him which your husband will not recognize and—"

"For Heaven's sake, make an end of it!" The old gentleman brought his fist down angrily on the window-sill. "Do you want to give her the poison drop by drop?"

He took Gertrude's hand again, and tried to find words to explain.

"You see, Gertrude, it is not so bad; it often happens, and this Wolff may have thrust himself forward, in short—he is a sort of a walking encyclopædia, knows everybody hereabouts, and whenever any one wants to know anything he is sure to be able to tell him. So your husband—well, how shall I excuse it?—he inquired about your circumstances, do you understand?—before he offered himself to you—*voilà tout.* It happens hundreds of times, child, and you are reasonable, Gertrude, aren't you ? "

The young wife stood motionless as a statue. Only gradually the color came to her cheeks.

"That is a lie !" she cried, drawing a long breath. " Did you bring me here for *that* ? "

" But Wolff was here," moaned Mrs. Baumhagen, " asking for my intervention."

" No, he came to *us*," corrected Jenny, "early this morning ; he wanted to speak to Arthur, but Arthur—" she hesitated, "last evening Arthur— "

" You may as well say that Arthur started off suddenly on a journey in the night," interposed Mrs. Baumhagen sharply, " I am very fortunate in my children's marriages ! "

" Well, I can't help it if he gets angry at every little thing," laughed the young wife, quite undisturbed. " Besides we are very happy."

" A pretty kind of happiness," grumbled the old gentleman to himself, so low that no one but Gertrude could hear it. Then he added aloud, " A hurried journey on business, we will call it, a sudden journey on business, preceded by a little curtain lecture."

"Oh, to be sure, a journey on business," said Mrs. Baumhagen in a tone of pique, "to Manchester."

"What has that got to do with Gertrude's affairs?" asked Uncle Henry. "It is enough that Arthur was not there, and the gentleman went up another flight and spoke to your mother, my child. It is not worth mentioning —if I had only been here sooner. It is very disagreeable that you should have heard of it, but believe me, my child, they all do it now-a-days."

The good-natured little man clapped her kindly on the shoulder.

Mrs. Baumhagen, however, started up like an angry lioness.

"Don't talk such nonsense! How can you smooth it over? It was nothing but a common swindle. I hope Gertrude has enough sense of dignity to tell Mr. Linden that—"

"Not another word!"

The young wife stood almost threatening before her in the middle of the room.

"But for mercy's sake! It will be the most scandalous case that was ever known," sobbed

the excited lady. "He is going to sue Linden—you will both have to appear in court."

Gertrude did not utter a syllable.

" Have the kindness to order a carriage,
uncle," she entreated.

"No, you must not go away so! you look
shockingly," was the anxious cry of her
mother and sister.

" Do listen to reason, Gertrude," said
Jenny in a complaining tone.

" We must silence Wolff—uncle can inquire
how much he asks for his services, and—"

"And you will come to us again," sobbed
her mother. "Gertrude, Gertrude, my poor
unhappy child, did I not foresee this ?"

"This is too much !" growled the old
gentleman. "Confound these women ! Don't
let them talk you into anything, child," he
cried, forcibly; "settle it with your husband
alone."

" A carriage, uncle," reiterated the young
wife.

"Wait a while at least," entreated Jenny,
" till mamma's lawyer—"

"Oh," groaned Uncle Henry, "if Arthur
had only been here, this confounded affair

wouldn't have been left in the women's hands. I will get you a carriage, Gertrude. Your nags are at the factory, Jenny? Very well. Excuse me a moment."

Gertrude was standing in the window like one stunned; she had as yet no clear understanding of the matter. "The whole city is talking about it," she heard her mother sob. Of what then? She tried forcibly to collect her thoughts, but in vain. Only one thing: it is not true! went over and over in her mind.

She clenched her little hand in its leather glove. "A lie! A lie!" fell again from her lips. But this lie had spread itself like a heavy mist over her young happiness, bringing so much vague alarm that her breath came thick and fast.

"Shall I go with you?" asked Jenny. The carriage was just coming across the square.

"No, thank you. I require no third person between my husband and myself."

Her words sounded cold and hard.

"You look so miserable," groaned her mother.

"Then the sooner I get home the better."

"At least send back a messenger at once."

"Perhaps you think he beats me too?" she inquired, ironically, turning to go.

"Child! child!" cried Mrs. Baumhagen, stretching out her arms towards her, "be reasonable, don't be so blind where facts speak so loudly."

But she did not turn back. Calmly she took down her mantle from the hat-stand. Sophie gazed anxiously into the pale, still face of the young wife, who quite forgot to say a pleasant word to the old servant. At the carriage-door stood Uncle Henry.

"Let me go with you, Gertrude," he entreated.

She shook her head.

"It is only out of pure selfishness, Gertrude," he continued. "If I don't know how it is going with you I shall be ill."

"No, uncle. We two require no one; we shall get on better alone."

"Don't break the staff at once, child," he said, gently.

"I do not need to do that, Uncle Henry."

He lifted his hat from his bald head. There was a reverent expression in his eyes.

"Good-bye, Gertrude, little Gertrude. If I had had my way, you would not have heard a word of it."

She bent her head gravely.

"It is best so, uncle."

Then she went back the way she had come.

The rain beat against the rattling panes and dashed against the leather top of the carriage, and they went so slowly. The young wife gazed out into the misty landscape. The splendor of the blossoms had vanished, the white petals were swimming in the pools in the streets.

"Oh, only one sunbeam!" she thought, the weather oppressed and weighed her down so.

Absurd! How could any one be so influence by foolish gossip! Mamma always looked on the dark side of everything—and even if she always told the truth, she had been imposed upon by this story. Poor Frank! Now there would be vexation—the first! She would tell him of it playfully—after dinner, when they were alone together, then she would

13

say, "Frank, I must tell you something that will make you laugh. Just fancy, you have a very bitter enemy, and his revenge is so absurd, he declares "—she was smiling now herself—" Yes, that is the way it shall be."

She was just passing the old watch tower. What was she thinking of as she passed this place a few hours before? Oh yes—a crimson flush spread over her countenance—of the cradle in the attic. She could see the old cradle so plainly before her; two red roses were painted on one end, in the middle a golden star, and beneath it stood written : "Happy are they who are happy in their children."

She put her hand in her pocket and took out the note-book—the carriage was crawling so slowly up the hill—she could not remember it all yet, she must read the verses again.

It was a vision he had had of her kneeling before a cradle, singing a cradle-song about the father bringing something home to his son from the green wood.

She let the paper fall. She knew what song he meant—the old nursery song that she had

been singing to her godchild when he had
heard her from the window outside. He had
told her about it and that in that moment he
had come quite under her spell.

She pressed the book to her lips. Ah, how
far beneath her seemed envy and spite! how
powerless they seemed before the expectation
of such happiness!

Just then a piece of paper fell down, a piece
of blue writing-paper. She picked it up; it
was part of a letter on the blank side of which
was written in Frank's handwriting:

"Half a hundred-weight grass-seed, mixed,"
with the address of a manufactory of farming
utensils.

She turned it over, looked at it carelessly,
then suddenly every trace of color left her
face. She raised her eyes with a scared expression in them, then looked down again—
yes, there it was!

"—— Besides the above-mentioned property Miss Gertrude Baumhagen owns a villa
near Bergedorf. A massive building, splen-
didly furnished, with stables, gardener's house
and a garden-lot of ten acres, partly wood,
enclosed by a massive wall.

" The property is recorded in the name of the young lady, being valued at twenty-four thousand dollars.

" For any further details I am quite at your service.

　　　" Very respectfully yours,

　　　　　　" C. Wolff, Agent.

D. 21 Dec. 1882.

Gertrude tried to read it again, but her hand trembled so violently that the letters danced before her eyes. She had seen it, however, distinctly enough; it would not change read it as often as she might. With pitiless certainty the conviction forced itself upon her: it is the truth, the horrible truth! and every word of his had been a lie.

She had been bought and sold like a piece of merchandise—she, *she* had been caught in such a snare!

She had taken *that* for love which had been only the commonest mercenary speculation.

Ah, the humiliation was nothing to the dreadful feeling that stole over her and chilled her to the heart—the pain of wounded pride and with it the old bitter perversity. She had not felt it lately, she had been good, happiness makes one so good—and now? and now?

CHAPTER XIII.

THE carriage rolled quickly down the hill to Niendorf and stopped before the house. Half-unconsciously the young wife descended and stood in the rain on the steps of the veranda. It seemed to her as if she were here for the first time; the small windows, the gray old walls with the pointed roof—how ugly they were, how strange! All the flowers in the garden beaten down by the rain—the charm that love gives fled, only bare, sober, sad reality! and on the threshold crouched the demon of selfishness, of cold calculation.

She passed through the garden hall and up the stairs to her room. In the corridor Johanna met her.

"The master went away in the carriage directly after breakfast," she announced. "He laid a note on your work-table, ma'am."

"I have a headache, Johanna, don't disturb me now," she said, faintly.

When she reached her own room she bolted first the door behind her and then that which opened into his room. And then she read the note.

"The barometer has risen and the judge insists on going up the Brocken. I go with him to Ille. I have something to do there and I shall not be very late home—Thine,

FRANK."

And below a postscript from the guest:

"Don't be angry, Mrs. Linden. I belong to that class of persons who cannot see a mountain without feeling an irresistible desire to ascend it. I take the Brocken first, so when the weather clears again I can bear the sight of it from my window with equanimity. I will send your Frank home again soon, safe and sound."

Thank Heaven, he would not be back so very soon—but what was to be done now? She sat motionless before her work-table, gazing out into the garden without seeing anything there. Hour after hour passed. Once or twice she passed her hand across her eyes —they were dry and hot, and about the mouth was graven a deep line of scorn and contempt.

Towards evening there was a knock at the door. She did not turn her head.

" Mrs. Linden ! " called the servant. No answer and the steps died away outside.

Gertrude Linden got up then and went to her writing-desk. Calmly she opened the pretty blotting-book, drew up a chair, grasped a pen and seated herself to write. She had thought of it long enough ; without hesitation the words flowed from her pen :

" I will beg Uncle Henry to explain everything to you as gently as possible. I cannot speak of it myself—it is the most painful disappointment of my whole life. I only ask you at present to confirm my own declaration that I must live in retirement for some time on account of my health. It will not take long to decide upon something.   GERTRUDE."

She sealed the note and put it on the writing table in her husband's room. She put the packet of poems beside it and the note-book also. What should she do with it? The poem was nothing to her—it was only an old habit of his to write verses ; the judge had let that out yesterday. He had only made use of it in this case as a useful means for making the deception complete. A man who writes tender verses while at the same time he is privately acquainting himself with the amount of the lady's fortune through an agent —that was a tragi-comedy indeed, that would make a good plot for a farce—and *she* was to be the heroine !

She kept the fragment of that dreadful letter. Then she wrote a note to her mother and one to Uncle Henry, then took out her watch and looked for a time-table.

Whither? The Berlin express which connected them with all the outer world was already gone. Then she must wait until to-morrow—and then? Somewhere she must go —she must be alone! Only not with mamma and Jenny, somewhere far away from here.

She suddenly sprang up with startled eyes, she heard a voice, his voice.

" Has my wife come back ? "

Then a merry whistle, a few bars from " Boccaccio " and hasty steps in the corridor. Now his hand was on the door-knob. It was locked.

" Gertrude! " he called.

She was standing in the middle of the room,

her lips pressed together, her eyes stretched wide open, but she did not stir.

He supposed she was not there and went quietly into his own room. She heard him open the door of the bedroom.

"Gertrude!" he called again.

Back into his own room; he spoke to the dog, whistled a few bars of his opera-air again, moved about here and there and then stopped—now he was tearing a paper—now he was reading her note.

"Gertrude, Gertrude, I know you are in your room. Open the door!"

His voice sounded calm and kind, but she stood still as a statue.

"Please open the door!" now sounded authoritatively.

"No," she answered loudly.

"You are laboring under some horrible mistake! Some one has been telling you something—let me speak to you, child!"

"She came a step nearer.

"I cannot," she said.

"I must entreat you to open the door. Even a criminal is heard before he is condemned."

"No," she declared, and went to the window, where she remained.

"Confound your—obstinacy," sounded in her ears.

Then a crash, a splitting of wood—the door was burst open and Frank Linden stood on the threshold.

"Now I demand an explanation," he said angrily, the swollen veins standing out on his white forehead, which formed a strange contrast to his brown face.

She did not turn towards him.

"Uncle Henry will tell you what there is to tell," she replied, coldly.

He strode up to her and laid his hand on her shoulder, but she drew back, and the blue eyes, usually so soft, looked at him so coldly and strangely that he started back, deeply shocked.

"I have deceived you, Gertrude? you, Gertrude?" he asked, "what have I done? What is my crime?"

"Nothing—"

"That is no answer, Gertrude."

"Oh, it is only such a trifle—I cannot talk to you about it."

"Very well! Then I will go to Uncle Henry at once."

She made no answer.

"And you wish to go away? To leave me alone?" he inquired again.

She hesitated a moment.

"Yes, yes," she then said, hastily, "away from here."

"Why do you keep up this farce, Gertrude."

"Farce?" She laughed shortly.

"Gertrude, you hurt me."

"Not more than you have hurt me."

"But, confound it, I ask you—how?" he cried in fierce anger.

She had drawn back a little and looked at him with dignity.

"Pray, order the carriage and go to Uncle Henry,". she replied, coldly.

"Yes, by Heaven, you are right," he cried, quite beside himself, "you are more than perverse!"

"I told you so before; it is my character."

"Gertrude," he began, "I am easily aroused, and nothing angers me so much as passive opposition. It is our duty to have trust in one another—tell me what troubles you; it *can* be explained. I am conscious of no wrong done to you."

"That is a matter of opinion," said she.

"Very well. I declare to you that I am not in the least curious—and I give you time to reconsider."

He turned to go.

"That is certainly the most convenient thing to do in this matter," she retorted, bitterly.

He hesitated, but he went nevertheless, closed the broken door behind him as well as he could and began to walk up and down his room.

She pressed her forehead against the window-pane and gazed out into the garden. It had stopped raining; the clouds were lifting in the west and displaying gleams of the setting sun. Then the heavy masses of fog broke away and at the same moment the landscape blazed out in brilliant sunshine like a beautiful woman laughing through her tears.

If *she* could only weep! They who have a capacity for tears are favored. Weeping makes the heart light, the mood softer—but there were no tears for her.

CHAPTER XIV.

In the late twilight the iron-gray horses stopped before the door and Jenny got out of the carriage.

She ran lightly as a cat up the veranda steps and suddenly stood in the garden-hall before Frank Linden, who sat at the table alone. Gertrude's plate was untouched.

"So late, Jenny?" he asked.

"I want to speak to Gertrude."

"You will find my—wife in her room."

Jenny cast a quick glance at him from her bright eyes. Had the blow fallen? She had nearly died of anxiety at home.

"Is not Gertrude well?" she inquired, innocently.

He hesitated a moment.

"She seems rather excited and tired. I thing something has happened to disturb her in the course of the day."

"Ah, indeed!" said Mrs. Fredericks. "Well, I will go and see her myself."

She passed through the hall. The lamp was not yet lighted and in the darkness she stumbled over something and nearly fell. As she uttered a slight cry, Johanna hastened in with a light.

"Oh, I beg your pardon, ma'am, it is the young lady's trunk, who arrived about a quarter of an hour ago. Dora forgot to carry it to her room."

Jenny cast an angry glance at the modest box, ran up the stairs and knocked at her sister's door.

"It is I, Gertrude," she called out in her clear ringing voice. She heard light footsteps and the bolt was gently drawn back and the door opened.

"You, Jenny?" inquired Gertrude, just as Frank had said a few minutes before, "you, Jenny?"

It was almost dark in the room; Jenny could not see her sister's face.

"Why do you sit here in the dark, Gertrude? I beg of you tell me quick all that has happened. Mamma and I are dying of anxiety."

"You need have no anxiety," replied Gertrude. "It is all right."

"All right?" asked Jenny in surprise. "You cannot make me believe that. *He* alone at the table and *you* up here with your door locked—come confess, child, that you have not made it up."

"Please take a seat, Jenny," said the young wife, wearily.

Jenny sat down on the lounge, and Gertrude took up her position at the window again. It was still as death in the room and in the whole house.

"It would have been wiser if you had not married at all, Gertrude," began her sister, with a sigh.

"But, it can't be helped—you are tied fast —oh, yes! You must put up with everything, you must not even have an opinion of your own. I am quite ill too from the vexation I had last evening. At last I ran up to mamma. She was dreadfully frightened when she saw me standing before her bed in my night-dress. I cried all night long. This morning I waited.

I thought he would come up for me, he was usually so remorseful—but he didn't come and as I was taking breakfast with mamma Sophie brought me a card from him in which he very coolly informed me that he had gone to Manchester for a fortnight. Well—I wish him a happy journey!"

Gertrude made no reply.

"You must not take it so dreadfully to heart, child," continued the young matron. "Good gracious, it is well it is no worse. All women have something to put up with and sometimes it is far worse than this."

"Have they?" asked Gertrude, in a low voice.

"Yes, of course!" cried Jenny, in surprise.

"Do you think a woman can take up her bundle and march off? Bah! Then no woman would stay with her husband a moment. No, no,—people get reconciled to one another and they just take the first opportunity to pay each other off. That is always great fun for me. Just you see, pet, how good Arthur will be when he comes back; for a whole month he will be the nicest husband in the world."

"That would be an impossibility for me,"
cried Gertrude, clearly and firmly. "To-day
bitter as death, to-morrow fondly loving; it is
simply shameful."

Jenny was silent.

"Good gracious," she said at length, yawning, "one is as good as the other! If I were
to separate from Arthur,—who knows but I
might get a worse one! For of course I
should marry again, what else can a woman
do? By the way, mamma spoke to the lawyer—he urgently advised her to hush up the
matter as well as possible. Mamma thought
differently, but Mr. Sneider declared—you see
now, one *can't* get away even if one wants to—
that there were no grounds for a divorce, and
I said to mamma too, 'Gertrude,' said I,
'leave him? Incredible! She is dead in
love with the man. He might have murdered
somebody, I really believe, and she would
still find excuses for him.' Was I right?"

Gertrude suffered tortures. She wrung her
hands in silence and her eyes were fixed on
the dark sky above her in which the evening
star was now sparkling with a greenish light.
Jenny yawned again.

14

"Ah, just think," she continued, "you don't know what we quarrelled about, Arthur and I. He reproached me with spending too much on my dress; of course that was only a pretext to give vent to his ill temper—there were business letters very likely containing bad news. I replied that did not concern him, I did not inquire into his expenses. Then he was cross and declared that I had tried in Nice to copy the dresses of the elegant French women. But it is not true, for I only bought two dresses there. Gracious, yes, they were rather dearer than if my dressmaker in Berlin had made them. Of course I said again, 'That is not your affair, for I pay for them.' Then he talked in a very moral strain about honorable women and German women who helped to increase the prosperity of a house. Other fortunes besides ours had been thrown away and when the truth was known it was always the fault of 'Madame.' He found fault with mamma for making herself so ridiculous with her youthful costumes, and at last he declared we owed some duty to our future children —Heaven preserve me! I have had to give

up my poor sweet little Walter, and I will
have no more. The pain of losing him was too
great; I should die of anxiety. In short, he
played the part of a real provincial Philistine,
and finally even that of Othello, for he declared Col. von Brelow always had such a
confidential air with me. That was too much
for my patience. I proposed that we should
separate then. You understand I only said
so—for he is pretty obedient generally, when
I hold the reins tight. And as I said before
one can't get free for nothing. 'I will go
at once!' I cried, and then I ran up to
mamma."

"Stop, I beg of you," cried Gertrude,
hastily rising. She rang for a light and
when Johanna brought the lamp it lighted up
a feverish face, and eyes swollen as if with
burning tears, and yet Gertrude had not wept.

"How you look, child," remarked Jenny.
"Well, and what is to be done now? I must
tell mamma something, it was for that I
came."

She cast a glance at the dainty time-piece
above the writing-table.

"Five minutes to nine—I must be going

home. Do tell me how you mean to arrange matters?"

"You shall hear to-morrow—the day after to-morrow—I don't know yet," stammered the young wife, pressing her hand on her aching head.

"Only don't make a scandal, Gertrude," and Jenny took up her gray cloak with its red silk lining and tied the lace strings of her hat.

" If the affair is settled as Mr. Sneider advises, it is the best you can do. By the way, how does Frank take it? Has he confessed it? To be sure, what else could he do? Well, let me hear to-morrow then, at latest. By the way, child, it has just occurred to me —that day that Linden called on us the first time, that fellow, that Wolff, came with him across the square to our house. I was sitting in the bay-window and I was surprised to see how confidentially Wolff clapped him on the shoulder."

Gertrude stood motionless. Ah, she had seen the same thing ; she recalled it so clearly at this moment.

"Yes, yes," she stammered.

" The lawyer says he does a great deal of that sort of business. But now good-night, my pet—will you send in word or shall we send some one out in the morning ? "

" I will send word," replied Gertrude.

She did not go out with her sister, she stood still in her place, her head sunk on her breast, her arms hanging nerveless by her side. This conversation with Jenny had opened an abyss before her eyes; she no longer knew what she should do, only one thing was clear, she could not stay with him ; she could not endure a life of indifference by his side, and—any other life would never again be possible to them. " Never ! " she said aloud with decision, " Never ! "

She heard his steps now in the next room ; then the steps went away again and presently she heard them on the gravel-walk in the garden till they finally died away. She was so tired and it was so cold, and she could not realize that there had ever been a time when it had been different,—when she had been happy—she seemed to herself so degraded.

She had that fatal letter still in her hand, where it burnt like glowing coals. She knew an old maid, the daughter of a poor official, who was soured and embittered. For thirteen years she had been engaged to a poor referendary, and finally they had recognized the fact that they never would be rich enough to marry. She had remained lonely and pitied by all who knew her history.

Ah, if she could only have exchanged with her, who had been loved for her own sake! And even if she could forgive him for not having loved her, the lie, the hypocrisy she could never forgive—never, never. Her faith in him was gone.

Half unconsciously she had wandered out into the corridor, and felt a little refreshed by the cooler air. She ran quickly down the steps into the garden. From the kitchen came the sounds of talking and laughing; the gardener was talking nonsense to the maids— the mistress' eye was wanting.

There was no light in the garden-hall, but Aunt Rosa's windows were unusually brilliant and a youthful shadow was marked out on the white curtain. That must be the expected niece.

Gertrude walked on in the gravel-walks; the

nightingales were singing and there were sounds of singing in the steward's room, a deep sympathetic tenor and a sorrowful melody.

On and on she went in the fragrant garden. Then she cried out suddenly,

" Frank ! "

She had come upon him suddenly at a turning of the path.

" Gertrude ! " returned he, trying to take her hand.

" Don't touch me ! " she cried. " I was not looking for you, but as we have met, I will ask you for something."

In order to support herself she clutched the branches of a lilac-bush with her little hand.

" With all my heart, Gertrude," he replied gently. " Forgive my violence, anger catches me unawares sometimes. I promise you it shall not happen again."

He stopped, waiting to hear her request. For a while they stood there in silence, then she spoke slowly, almost unintelligibly in her great agitation. " Give me my freedom again —it is impossible any longer to— "

" I do not understand you," he replied, coldly, " what do you mean ? "

" I will leave you everything, everything—
only give me my freedom! We cannot live
together any longer, don't you see that ? " she
cried quite beside herself.

" Speak lower ! " he commanded, stamping
angrily with his foot.

" Say yes ! " entreated the young wife with
a voice nearly choked with emotion.

" I say no ! " was the answer. " Take my
arm and come."

" I will *not !* I will not ! " she cried, snatch-
ing away her hand which he had taken.

" You are greatly excited this evening, you
will come now into the house with me ; to-
morrow we will talk further on the subject
and in the clear daylight you can tell me what
reasons you have for thinking our living together impossible."

" Now, at once, if you wish it ! " she gasped
out. " Because two things are wanting, two
little trifling things only,—trust and esteem !
I will not speak of love—you have not been
true to me, Frank, you have deceived me and
lost my confidence. Let me go, I entreat
you, for the love of Heaven—let me go ! "

As he made no reply, she went on rapidly.

her words almost stumbling over each other
so fast they came. " I know that I have no
right in law; people would laugh at a woman
who demanded her freedom on no better
grounds than that she had been lied to once.
So I come as a suppliant; be so very good as
to let me go, I cannot bear to live with you in
mistrust and—and— "

" Come, Gertrude," he said, gently, "you
are ill. Come into the house now and let us
talk it over in our room—come ! "

" Ill—yes ! I wish I might die," she murmured.

Then she suddenly grew calm and went
back into the house with him. He opened
the door of his room and she went in, but she
passed quickly through into her own, threw
herself on her lounge, drew the soft coverlid
over her and closed her eyes. Frank stood
helpless before her.

" I will have a cup of tea made for you,"
said the young man, kindly.

She looked unspeakably wretched, as she
lay there, the long black lashes resting like
dark shadows on her white cheeks. She
must have suffered frightfully.

"Go to bed, Gertrude," he begged anxiously, "it will be better for you and tomorrow we will talk about this."

" I shall stay here," she replied decisively, turning her head away.

Then he lost patience.

"Confound your silly obstinacy ! " he cried angrily.   " Do you think I am a foolish boy ? I will show you how naughty children ought to be treated ! "

Then he turned and banging the door after him he went away.

CHAPTER XV.

THE first rays of the morning sun were resting like reddish gold on the tips of the forest trees which crowded close up to the white villa-like house. Magnificent oaks, like giant sentinels, stood on the lawn before the massive wall. A narrow, little-used path wound in between them, such as are to be found in places not intended to be walked upon. The great trees gave out little shade as yet, the oak-tree is late in getting its leaves; those that had already appeared looked young and shrivelled against the knotted branches, and formed a delightful contrast to the dark green of the evergreens on the other side of the garden wall, mingled with the tender misty foliage of the birches. "Waldruhe" lay as if dreaming in this early stillness. The green jalousies were all closed, like sleepy eyelids; on the roof a row of bright-feathered pigeons were sunning themselves. The lawn before the house was like a wilderness, the grass-grown paths scarcely distinguishable, which led from the great iron gate to the veranda steps. From a side-building a little smoke rose up to the blue sky, and a cat sat crouched on the wooden bench beside the hall-door. There was no sound except the joyful trills of the larks as they soared out of sight in the blue sky.

From under the oaks a slender woman's figure drew near. She walked slowly, and her eyes glanced now to the left over the green wheat fields to the open country, and now rested on the trees beside her. She must have come a long way, for the delicate face looked worn and weary, dark shadows were under her eyes, and the bottom of her dress was damp as were also the small shoes which peeped out under the gray woollen robe. She went straight up to the iron gate, clasped the rusty bars with her ungloved hands and looked at the house somewhat in the attitude of an curious child, but her eyes were too grave for that. Beside her stood a brown dog wagging his tail, raising inquiringly his shrewd eyes to her face, but she took no heed

"SHE LEANED WITH HER UNGLOVED HANDS AGAINST THE MISTY BARS OF THE GATE."

Page 240.

of the animal that had followed her so faithfully. Her thoughts took only one direction.

She had never been here since that day when she had run hither in desperate fear, to arrive—only too late. Everything was the same now as then—just as lonely and deserted. She pulled the bell, how hard it pulled! Ah, no hand had touched it since!

It is true Sophie came here conscientiously every spring and every autumn to beat the furniture and air the rooms, but no one else. Mrs. Baumhagen had from the first declared this idyllic whim of her husband's an absurdity, and Jenny always called the country house "Whim Hall." She had been here once but would never come again, "one would die of ennui among those stupid trees."

At length the bell gave out a faint tinkle. Thereupon arose a fierce barking in the side-building and a woman of some fifty years in a wadded petticoat and a red-flannel bed-gown came out of the house. She stared at the young lady in amazement, then she clapped her hands together and ran back into the house with her slippers flapping at each step, returning presently with a bunch of keys.

"Merciful powers!" cried she as she opened the door, "I can't believe my own eyes—Mrs. Linden! Have you been taking a morning walk, ma'am? I've always wondered if you wouldn't come here some day with your husband—and now here you are —and that is a pleasure to be sure!" And she ran before, opening the doors.

"It is all in order, Mrs. Linden—my man always insists upon that—'Just you see,' he says, 'some day some of the ladies will be popping in on you.'" And the square little body ran on again to open a door. "It is all as it used to be—there is your bed and there are the books, only the evergreens and the beeches have grown taller."

The young wife nodded.

"Bring me a little hot milk," she said, shivering, "as soon as you can, Mrs. Rode."

"This very minute!" And the old woman hurried away. Gertrude could hear the clatter of her slippers on the stairs and the shutting of the hall door. At last she was alone.

A cool green twilight reigned in the room from the branches of the beeches which pressed close up to the pane. It was not so dark here that last summer she had spent in "Waldruhe." Otherwise—the woman was right—everything was as it had been then, the mirror in its pear-wood frame still displayed the Centaurs drawing their bows in the yellow and black ground of the upper part; above the small old-fashioned writing-table still hung the engraving, "Paul and Virginia" under the palm trees; the green curtains of the great canopied bed were not in the least faded, the sofa was as uncomfortable as ever, and the table stood before it with the same plush cover. She had passed so many pleasant hours here, in the sweet spring evenings at the open window, and on stormy autumn evenings when the clouds were flying in the sky, the storm came down from the mountains and beat against the lonely house. The rain pattered against the panes, and the woods began to rustle with a melancholy sound. Then the curtains were drawn, the fire burned brightly in the fireplace, and opposite in the cosy sitting-room her father sat at a game of cards. She was the hostess here in "Waldruhe," and she felt so proud of going into the kitchen with her white apron on and of going down into the cellar, and then at dinner all the old gentlemen complimented her on the success of her venison pie. The dear old friends—there was only Uncle Henry left now.

There on that bed they had laid the fainting girl when they had found her by her father's death-bed.

The young wife shivered suddenly. "He died of his unhappy marriage," she had once heard Uncle Henry say—in a low tone, but she had understood him nevertheless.

Mamma did not love him, she had loved another man, and she had told him so once, when they were quarreling about some trifle.

"I should have been happier with the other one—I liked him at any rate, but—he was poor."

Gertrude understood it all now; she had her father's character, she was proud, too. Oh, those gloomy years when she was growing to understand what sunshine was wanting in the house !

"If it were not for the children," he had said once, angrily, "I would have put an end to it long ago."

. O what a torture it is when two people are bound together by the law of God and man who would yet gladly put a whole world between them! Unworthy? Immoral?

Had not her father done well when he went voluntarily? But ah, how hard was the going when one loves! How then? Love and esteem belong together—ah, it was imagination, all imagination!

She grew suddenly a shade paler; she thought how her father had loved her and she thought of the little cradle in the attic at home. Thank God, it was only a dream, a wish, a nothing, and yet—Oh, this sickening dread!

She went towards the bed, she was so tired; she nestled her head in the pillow, drew up the coverlid and closed her eyes. And then she seemed to be always seeing and hearing the words that she had written to-day to leave on his writing-table. And she murmured, "Have compassion on me, let me go! Do not follow me, leave me the only place that belongs to me!"

The housekeeper brought some hot milk and she drank it. She would go to sleep, she

15

said, but she could not sleep. She was
always listening ; she thought she heard horses'
hoofs and carriage wheels. Ah, not that, not
that !

Hour after hour passed and still she lay
motionless ; she had no longer the strength to
move. Why can one not die when one
will ?

The noon-day bell was ringing in the village
when a carriage drove up and soon after steps
came up the stairs.

Thank God, it was not he !

Uncle Henry put his troubled face in at the
door.

"Really," he said, "you are here then !
But why, child, why ? "

She had risen hastily and now stood before
the little old gentleman.

"You bring me an answer, uncle ? "

"Yes, to be sure. But I would rather far
do something else. How happens it that your .
precious set should choose me for your amiable messenger ? "

He threw himself down on the sofa with
such force that it fairly groaned under his
weight.

" Have you any cognac here ? " he inquired,
" I am quite upset."

She shook her head without speaking and
only gazed at him with gloomy eyes.

" No, I suppose not," grumbled Uncle
Henry. " Well then, he says if it amuses you
to stay here you are quite welcome to do so."

She started perceptibly.

" Oh, ta, ta ! That is the upshot of it—
about that," he continued, wiping his forehead
with his handkerchief.

" Linden did not say much," he went on,
" he was in a silent rage over your flight—
however, he kept himself well in hand. He
would not keep you, he said, nor would he
drag you back to his house by force. He will
send Johanna to wait on you, and hopes to be
able to fulfil any other desire of yours. He
will arrange everything—and it is to be hoped
you will soon see your error. And," wound
up Uncle Henry, " now that we have got so
far, I should be glad to learn from you what is
to happen, when you, with your well known
obstinacy, do not feel inclined to own yourself wrong ? "

She was silent.

"As for the rest, Frank utterly denies having had any connection with Wolff. And, I should like to know, Gertrude—you were always a reasonable woman—why have you taken it into your head to believe that old ass who was always known as a scoundrel, rather than your husband?"

Gertrude quickly put her hand in her pocket and grasped the letter—there was her proof. She made a motion to give it to him—but no, she could not do it, she could not bring out the small hand that had closed tightly over the fatal paper.

"You ought both of you to give way a little, I think," said Uncle Henry after awhile. "You are married now, and—*au fond*—what if he did inquire about your fortune?"

Her frowning glance stopped him.

"Now-a-days it is not such a wonderful thing if a man—" he stammered on.

"It is not that, it is not that, uncle! Stop, I beg of you!" cried Gertrude.

"Oh yes, I understand, women are more sensitive in such matters, and justly too," assented Uncle Henry. "Well, I fear the name of Baumhagen will be the talk of the

town again for the next six months. Good-
bye, Gertrude. I can't exactly say I have
enjoyed my visit. Don't be too lonely."

At the door he turned back again.

" You know it will come before the courts.
Frank refuses to recognize the claims of the
fellow Wolff."

She shook her head.

" He will not refuse," she answered, calmly,
" but I wish you would take the matter in
hand, uncle, and pay Wolff for his trouble."

Her eyes filled suddenly with angry tears.

" Oh, ta, ta ! Why should I meddle with
the matter ? "

The old gentleman was deeply moved.

" I ask it of you, uncle, before it becomes
the talk of the town."

A sob choked her words.

" Ah, do you think, my child, it is not already whispered about ? Hm !—Well I will
do it, but entirely from selfish motives, you
know. Do you think it isn't disagreeable to
me, too ? Oh, ta, ta ! What big drops those
were ! But will you promise me then to let
well enough alone ! What ? You cannot
leave him ! "

The tears seemed frozen in her eyes.

"No," she replied, "but we shall agree upon a separation."

"Are you mad, child?" cried the old gentleman with a crimson face.

She turned her eyes slowly away.

"He only wanted my money; let him keep it," was her murmured reply. "*I* was only a necessary incumbrance,—*I!*"

"Oh, that is only your sensitiveness," said her uncle soothingly.

"Do you know me so little? she inquired, drawing herself up to her full height. Her swollen eyes looked into his with an expression of cold decision.

The little man hastily shut the door behind him. It was exactly as if his dead brother were looking at him. In a most uncomfortable frame of mind, he got into his carriage. Confound it! here he was plunged into difficulties again by his good nature.

Gertrude remained alone. For one moment she looked after him and then she covered her face with her hands despairingly, threw herself on the little sofa and wept.

CHAPTER XVI.

It was towards evening. Frank Linden mounted the steps, stood on the terrace and whistled shrilly out into the garden. He waited awhile and then shook his head. "The brute has gone with her," he said in a low voice; "even an animal like that takes part against me." He went back into the dining-room and stumbled over Johanna, who was busy at the side-board.

"You will go over to 'Waldruhe' in an hour," he said, looking past her. "Take what clothes are necessary for my wife with you. Whatever else she may desire is at her disposal at any moment."

Johanna glanced at him shyly, the face that was usually so glowing looked so ashy pale in the evening light.

"If I could have half an hour more, Mr. Linden—I want to show the young lady something about the milk cellar."

" The young lady ? ah—yes—"

" Yes, the young lady who came to visit Miss Rosa yesterday. She offered her services, sir, when she heard that Mrs. Linden had gone away. I don't know how I can manage without her either, Dora is so stupid and she has so much to do besides."

Before he could reply, the door opened softly and behind Aunt Rosa's wonderful figure appeared a dark girl with red cheeks and shining eyes, who when she perceived him made a rather awkward curtsy, and was at once introduced as Addie Strom.

Frank bowed to the ladies, stammered out a few civil words, and asked to be excused for leaving them as he had letters to write.

" I am so sorry," said Aunt Rosa, " that Mrs. Linden is not at home."

He nodded impatiently.

" She will soon be back," he replied as he went out.

" If Addie can help about the house a little —" sounded the shrill tones of the old lady behind him.

" Don't give yourself any trouble," was his reply.

"I should be glad to do it," said Adelaide, timidly.

Another silent bow from him and then he went out with great strides. That too!

He ran hastily down the steps into the garden. He took the letter out of his pocket once more which he had found lying on his writing-table that morning, and read it through. The writing was not as dainty as usual—the letters were hard and firm and large and yet unsteady, as if written, in great excitement.

The blood rushed in a hot wave to his heart. "It will come right." He put away the letter and took another from his pocket-book which had been brought half an hour before by an express messenger.

"I have just come from Wolff, with whom I intended to make an arrangement of this fatal affair. The scoundrel, unfortunately, was taken ill of typhus fever yesterday, and nothing is to be done with him at present. I can only regret that you should have consulted this man of all others, and I do not under-stand why you have not satisfied him. As soon as the gentleman is *au fait* again I shall take the liberty, in the interest of my family and especially of my niece, to settle the matter quietly, and beg you not to make the matter worse by any imprudence on your part. You must have some consideration for the family.

"May an old man give you a little advice? I am a very tolerant judge in this matter, but a woman thinks differently about it. Acknowledge the truth openly to your insulted little wife—with a person of her character it is the only way to gain her pardon. I will gladly do all in my power to set this foolish affair before her in the mildest light—"

" Consideration ! " he murmured, " consideration for the family ! "

Then he laughed aloud and went on more quickly into the deepening twilight. What should he do in the house, in the empty rooms, at the inhospitable table with his heart full of bitterness? Childish, foolish obstinacy it was in her—and no trust in him! How had he deserved that she should give him up at once without even hearing him? Well, she would get over it, she would come again, but—the spell was broken, the bloom, the freshness was gone.

He must have his rights without regard to the Baumhagen family, or to her on whom he would not have permitted the winds of heaven to blow too roughly. She could not have hurt him more, than by giving more credence to that scoundrel than to him—she who usually was so calm—calm?

He could see her eyes before him now, those eyes in which strong passion glowed. He had seen them blaze with anger more than once, he had heard her agitating sobs, her voice husky with emotion as she spoke of her father. He saw her again as she had been the evening before their marriage when she pressed his hands passionately to her lips, a mute eloquent gesture, a thanksgiving for the refuge of his breast. And now? It had already burned out this passionate love, had failed before the first trial.

It was already dark when he returned from his walk. Johanna was gone. The maid whom he met in the corridor told him she had taken her child and a trunk full of clothing and the books which had been sent to Mrs. Linden yesterday.

He went to her room; the sweet scent of violets of which she was so fond pervaded the atmosphere, the afghan on the lounge lay just as it had fallen when she threw it off as she rose. He could not stay—a longing for her seized upon him so powerfully that it well-nigh unmanned him, and he went back to the dining-room. He opened the door half-unconsciously—there sat the judge at the table, dusty and dishevelled from his Brocken tour, but contented to his inmost soul. But—how came this stranger here doing the honors?

The rosy little brunette was just setting the table. She had put on a white apron over her dark dress, the bib fastened smoothly across her full bust. She was just depositing with her round arm half-uncovered by the elbow-sleeve, a plate of cold meat by the judge's place, placing the bottle of beer beside it. And as she did so she laughed at the weary little man so that all her white teeth were displayed.

And this must he bear too, to make his comfort complete! Let them eat who would!

Soon he was sitting upstairs in the corner of the sofa in his own room; outside the darkness of a spring night came down, and a girl's voice was singing as if in emulation of the nightingales; that must be the little brunette, Adelaide. At last he heard it sounding up from the depths of the garden.

. He did not stir until the judge stood before him.

"Now, I should really like to know, Frank—are you bewitched or am I? What is the matter? Where is madame? The little black thing down-stairs, who seems to have fallen out of the clouds, says she is 'gone.'—Gone? What does it mean?"

"Gone!" repeated Frank Linden. It sounded so strange that his friend started.

"Something has happened, Frank,—that old woman, the mother-in-law, has done it. Oh, these women!"

"No, no, it is that affair with Wolff."

The judge gave vent to a long whistle, then he sat down beside Linden and clapped him on the shoulder.

"We'll manage *him*, Frank," he said, comfortingly, "and *she* will come back, she *must* come back; you will not even need to ask her. But it was the most foolish thing she could do to run away."

And he began to describe a case that had come up in Frankfort a short time before on the ground of wilful desertion.

Linden sprang up.

"Spare me your law cases," he said roughly. "Do you suppose I would bring her back by force?"

"And what if she will not come of herself, Frank?"

"She will come," he replied, shortly.

"And that scoundrel Wolff?"

Frank Linden gave his friend a cigar and took one himself, though he did not light it, and as he sat down again he said:

"You can ask that? Have I been in the habit of putting up with imposition, Richard?"

"No, but on what does the man found his claim?"

Frank shrugged his shoulders. "I told you before, that he declared when I turned him out, that he would know how to secure his rights. He is ill now, however," he added.

"Oh, that is fatal!" lamented the judge. He was silent, for just then the full, deep girl's voice came up from the garden:

> " Du hast mir viel gegeben,
> Du schenktest mir dein Herz,
> Du nahmst mir Alles wieder,
> Und liessest mir den Schmerz."

"It must be very hard, Frank," murmured his friend after a few moments of deep silence. "Very hard—I mean, to go the right way to work with a woman. How will you act? With sternness, or with gentleness? Will you write her a harsh letter, or will you send her some verses? In such an evening as this, I think I could almost write poetry myself. I say, Frank, light the lamp and let us read the paper."

"Richard," said the young man as he rose, "if you will give me your advice in regard to this affair of Wolff's, I shall be grateful to you, but leave my wife out of the question altogether; that is my affair alone."

CHAPTER XVII.

Mrs. Baumhagen had conquered her aversion to "Waldruhe" and had come to see her youngest daughter. Something must be done—at any rate she could not any longer endure the sympathetic inquiries for the health of the young Mrs. Linden. Something *must* be done.

Gertrude was sitting at the window reading in her cool dusky room, at least she held a book in her hand; at her feet lay Linden's dog. She started in dismay as she heard footsteps in the corridor and for one moment a deep flush spread over her face.

"Ah, mamma," she said, wearily, as Mrs. Baumhagen rustled in in a light gray toilet, her hat lavishly adorned with violets as being appropriate to half-mourning, the round face more deeply flushed than usual with the heat of the spring sun and her excitement.

"This can't go on any longer, child," she

began, kissing her daughter tenderly on the forehead. " How you look, and how cold it is here I Jenny sent her love ; she went to Paris this morning to meet Arthur. Why didn't you go too, as I proposed ? "

" I did not feel well enough," replied Gertrude.

" You look pale, and it is no wonder. I never could bear such want of consideration, either."

Gertrude sat down again in her old place.

" Has Uncle Henry been here ? " inquired Mrs. Baumhagen.

" He was here yesterday."

" Well, then, you know that Linden has forbidden him any interference with Wölff ? "

" Yes, mamma."

" And that this Mr. Wolff has been at the point of death for three days ? His death would be the best thing that could happen, for of course everything would come to an end then. I don't know whether the people in the city have any idea of the true state of the case, but they suspect something and they overwhelm me with inquiries about you."

16

Gertrude nodded slightly, she knew all that already from her uncle.

"And hasn't he been here? Did he not ask your pardon, has he not tried to get you back?" asked Mrs. Baumhagen, breathlessly.

"No," was the half-choked reply.

"Poor child!"

The mother pressed her cambric handkerchief to her eyes.

"It is brutal, really brutal! Thank God that your eyes have been opened so soon. But you cannot stay here the whole time before the separation?"

Gertrude started and looked at her mother with wide eyes. She herself had thought of nothing but a separation. But when she heard the dreadful word spoken, it fell on her like a thunderbolt.

"Yes," she said at length, wringing her hands nervously, "where should I stay?"

"And for pity's sake, what do you do here from morning till night?"

"I read and go to walk, and—" I grieve, she would have added, but she was silent. What did her mother know of grief!

"My poor child!"

Mrs. Baumhagen was really crying now. This atmosphere weighed on her nerves. There was something oppressive in the air, and they really had a dreadful time before them. What if he should not consent to a separation? Why had God given the child such an unbending will which had brought her into this misery! If she had only followed her mother's advice. Mrs. Baumhagen had taken an aversion to the man from the first moment.

"I think I must go home, my headache—" she stammered, unscrewing her bottle of smelling salts.

"If you want anything, Gertrude, write or send to me. Do you want a piano or books? I have Daudet's latest novel. Ah, child, there are many trials in life and especially in married life. You haven't experienced the worst of it yet."

"Thank you, mamma."

The young wife followed the mother down the corridor and down the stairs to the hall door. Mrs. Baumhagen said good-bye with a cheerful smile—the coachman need not know everything.

"I hope you will soon be better, Gertrude," she said, loudly. "Be persevering in your water-cure."

Gertrude, left alone, went on into the garden. At the end of the wall where the path curved was a little summer-house, with a roof of bark shaped like a mushroom. Here she stopped and looked out into the country which lay before her in all the glow and fragrance of the evening light. Behind the wooded hills of the Thurmberg stood the dear, cosy little house. She walked in spirit through all its rooms, but she forced her thoughts past one door, the room with the old mahogany furniture into which she had gone first on her wedding eve. And she leaned more firmly against the wall and gazed out at the setting sun which stood in the sky like a fiery red ball, till the tears streamed from her eyes, and her heart ached with mortification and humiliation. Why did that day always come back to her so, and that evening, the first in that room? The evening when she had slipped from his arms, down to his very feet, hiding her face in his hands, overwhelmed with her deep gratitude. Must he not have smiled to himself at the foolish, passionate, blindly credulous woman? And angry tears fell from her eyes down over her pale cheeks, her hands trembled, and her pride grew stronger every minute.

She turned and went back to the house, the dog still following, and when she reached her room she sat down on the ground like a child and put her arms round her brown companion's neck. She could weep now, she could cry aloud and no one would hear. Johanna had gone to Niendorf to get some books and all sorts of necessary things.

When Johanna came back at length, Gertrude sat in the corner of the sofa as quiet as ever. The lamp was lighted and she was reading. Johanna brought out a timid "Good evening!" which was acknowledged by a silent nod. She laid a few rosebuds down beside the book. "The first from the Niendorf garden, ma'am."

And when no answer came, she went on talking as she took the clothes out of the basket and packed them away in the wardrobe.

"Dora is gone, Mrs. Linden. She could not get on with Miss Adelaide, and the master packed her off. He is so angry. Mr. Baumhagen, who has just been there, complained bitterly of the dinner to-day. I was in the kitchen when he came in and said he had never eaten such miserable peas in his life and the ham was cut the wrong way. Then Miss Adelaide cried and complained, and declared she did it all only out of good-nature. And the judge tried to comfort her and said it was a pity to spoil her beautiful eyes.—The judge sent his compliments too, and said he would come to say good-bye to you, ma'am. He is going away in a few days. Mr. Baumhagen sent greetings too, and Miss Rosa and little Miss Adelaide—"

"Pray get the tea, Johanna," said the young lady, interrupting the stream of words.

"The milk was sour, too, ma'am, and it is so cool too. Ah, you ought to see the milk-cellar! Everything is going to ruin—it would really be better if you would only agree that Miss Adelaide should come here and let me go to the master."

"You will stay here," replied Gertrude, bending her eyes on her book.

"The master looks so pale," proceeded the

chattering woman. " Mr. Baumhagen was telling him in the garden-hall to-day that Wolff is dying, and he struck his hand on the table till all the dishes rattled and said, 'Everything goes against me in this matter!'"

Gertrude looked up. The color came back into her pale cheek, and she drew a long breath.

" Dying ? " she asked.

"Yes. I heard Mr. Baumhagen trying to soothe him—saying it was all for the best and he hoped everything might be comfortably settled now."

"What was my uncle doing there?" inquired Gertrude.

Johanna was embarrassed.

"I don't know, Mrs. Linden, but if I am not mistaken, he was trying to persuade Mr. Linden to — that — ah, ma'am ! "—Johanna came and stood before the table which she had set so daintily.

"What is between you and Mr. Linden I don't know, and it is none of my business to ask. But you see, ma'am, I have had a husband too, that I loved dearly—and life is so short, and I think we shouldn't make even one hour of it bitter, ma'am; the dead never come back again. But if I could know that my Fritz was still in the world and was sitting over there behind the hills, not so very far away from me—good Lord, how I would run to him even if he was ever so cross with me! I would fall on his neck and say, "Fritz, you may scold me and beat me, it is all one to me so long as I have you!"

And the young widow forgot the respect due to her mistress and threw a corner of her apron over her eyes and began to cry bitterly.

"Don't cry, Johanna," said Gertrude. "You don't understand—I too would rather it were so than that—" She stopped, overpowered by a feeling of choking anguish.

Johanna shook her head.

"'Taint right," she said, as she went out.

And Gertrude left the table and seated herself at the window, laying her forehead against the cool pane. Are not some words as powerful as if God himself had spoken them?

When some time after, Johanna entered the room again, she found it empty, and the table untouched. And as she began to remove the simple dishes, Gertrude entered and put a key down on the table. She had been in her father's room and the pale face with its frame of brown hair, looked as if turned to stone.

"If visitors come to-morrow, or at any time, I cannot receive them," she said, "unless it be my Uncle Henry."

And she took up her book again and began to read.

The house had long been quiet, when she put down the book for a moment and gazed into space.

"No!" she murmured, "no!"

CHAPTER XVIII.

THREE days later the Niendorf carriage stopped before the gate of "Waldruhe," and waited there a quarter of an hour in the blazing heat of the mid-day sun, so that the gardener's children could gaze to their heart's content on the brilliant coloring of Aunt Rosa's violet parasol and the red ostrich feathers which adorned Adelaide's summer hat, mingling effectively with the dark curly hair which hung in a fringe over the youthful forehead. This sight must have been an agreeable one to the judge also, for he did not take his eyes off his pretty *vis-à-vis*.

"Mrs. Linden regrets that she is not well enough to receive visitors," announced Johanna with her eyes cast down.

Two of the occupants of the carriage looked disappointed, while the judge felt in his pocket for his card-case.

" There ! " He gave the servant the turned-down card.

" And here is a letter, an *important letter*—do you understand, Johanna? My compliments, and I trust she will soon recover."

" So do I," said the young girl, timidly.

Aunt Rosa, however, was silent, and when they looked at her more closely they saw she was asleep, the wrinkled old face nodding absurdly above the enormous bow under her chin.

" Burmann, drive slowly, when we get to the wood," whispered the judge, " Miss Rosa is asleep."

The coachman made a clucking sound with his tongue and drove noiselessly over the soft grass-grown road. Johanna could see that the judge moved over from the middle of the seat opposite the young lady and that she glowed suddenly like the feathers on her hat.

Johanna went back into the house with her card and letter and gave them to Gertrude.

" A letter? " inquired the young wife.

" The judge gave it to me," replied Johanna,

as she left the room in which, in spite of the outside heat, the air was always damp and cold.

Gertrude slowly opened the letter. It was in his handwriting—she had expected it. Her heart beat so quickly she could scarcely breathe, and the letters danced before her eyes. It was some time before she could read it :

"GERTRUDE—Wolff died last evening. It is no longer possible to call him to account on earth; it is no longer possible to expose his guilt. He has gone to his grave without having cleared me from his calumny. I remain before you as a guilty person, and I can do nothing more than declare once more that we—you and I, are the victims of a scoundrel. I have never spoken with Wolff of your fortune nor called in his intervention in any way. I leave the rest to you and to your consideration. I shall never force you to return to me, neither shall I ever consent to a divorce. Come home, Gertrude, come soon and all shall be forgotten. The house is empty, and my heart is still more so—have faith in me again.   YOUR FRANK."

She had just finished reading these words when Uncle Henry came in. The little gentleman had evidently dined well—his face shone with good-humor.

"Still here?" he cried. And as she did not reply he looked at her more closely. "Well, you are not angry again?"

But the young wife swayed suddenly and Uncle Henry sprang towards her only just in time to keep her from falling, and called anxiously for Johanna. They laid the slender figure on the sofa and bathed her temples with cold water.

"Speak to me, child!" he cried, "speak to me!" and he repeated it till she opened her eyes.

"I cannot," she said after awhile.

"What?" asked the asthmatic old gentleman.

"Go to him I *can*not! Must I?"

"Merciful Heavens!" groaned Uncle Henry, "do be reasonable! Of course you must unless you want him to be ruined."

"I must?" she repeated, adding as if for her own comfort, "No, I must not! I cannot force myself to have confidence in him, I

cannot pretend what I do not feel.   No, I
must not!"

And she sprang up and ran through the
room to the door, trembling with excitement.

"Oh, ta, ta!"   The old man ran his hands
through his hair.   "Then stay here!   Let
your house and home go to ruin, and the husband to whom you have pledged your faith into
the bargain."

"Yes, yes," she murmured, "you are right,
but I cannot!"

And she grasped the little purse in her
pocket which held that fatal letter.

It seemed as if this brought her back at
once to herself.   She grew quiet, she lay back
on her lounge and rested her head on the
cushion.

"Pardon me, uncle—I know what I am
doing."

"That is **exactly** what you don't know," he
muttered.

"Yes, I do," was the pettish reply.   "Or
do you think I ought to go there and beg him
with folded hands to take me back into favor
again?"   And something like scorn curved
her lips.

"It would be the most sensible thing you could do," replied Uncle Henry, rather angrily.

She bent back her head proudly.

"No!" came from her lips, "not if I were still more miserable than I am! I can forgive him, but—fawn upon him like—like a hound —no!"

"God forgive me, but it is nothing but the purest arrogance that animates you," cried the old man. "Who gave you the right to set yourself so high above him? He was a poor man who could not marry without money—is it a crime that he should have asked a question as to this matter? It happens to every princess. You are stern and unloving and unjust. Have you never done anything wrong?"

She had started at his first reproachful words like a frightened child, now she sprang up and as she knelt down before him her eyes looked up at him imploringly.

"Uncle, do you know how I loved him? Do you know how a woman can love? I looked up to him as to the noblest being on earth, so lofty, so great he seemed to me. I have lain at his feet, and at night I folded my hands and thanked God that he had given me this man for my husband. I thought he was the only one who did not look on me only as a rich girl, and he has told me so a hundred times. Uncle, you have been always alone, you don't know how people can love! And then to come down and see in him only a common man, a man who does not disdain to tell a lie—O, I would rather have died!" And she hid her face in her trembling hands. "And there, where I have been so happy, shall I satisfy myself with the coldest duty? I must be his wife and know that it was not love that brought me to his side? I shall hear his tender words and not think, 'He does not mean them?' He will say something to me and I shall torment myself with doubts whether he really means it? Oh, hell itself could not be more dreadful, for I loved him!"

Tears stood in the old man's eyes. He stroked Gertrude's smooth hair in some embarrassment.

"Stand up, Gertrude," he said, gently; and after a pause he added, "The Bible says we shall forgive."

"Yes, with all my heart," she murmured. "And if you see him tell him so. Ah, if he had come and had said—'Forgive me '—but so—"

An idea came into Uncle Henry's head.

"Then would you give in, child?" he inquired.

"Yes," she stammered, "hard as it would be."

The old egotist knew then what he had to do. He led the weeping Gertrude to her little sofa, asked Johanna for a glass of wine and then drove to Niendorf. As he went he could see always before him the beautiful tear-stained face, and could hear her sad voice. As he ran up the steps to the garden-hall rather hastily he saw through the glass door the little brunette Adelaide sitting at the table with the judge, who was just uncorking a wine-bottle. Both were so deeply engaged in gazing at each other and blushing and gazing again that they were not conscious of the presence of the old spy outside.

"Really, this is a pretty time to be carousing in this house," thought Uncle Baumhagen. As he entered he brought the couple back to

17

the bald present with a gruff " Good morning,"
and the judge began at once a lament over
the horrible ill-luck of this Wolff's dying six
months too soon.

" What is going on here ? " asked Uncle
Henry, inhaling the fragrance of the wood-ruff.

" The parting *mai-trank* for the judge,"
replied Miss Adelaide.

" Oh, ta, ta! You are going away ? "

" I must," replied the little man with a re-
gretful look at the young girl. " Besides, my
dear sir, since this dreadful wifeless time has
begun it is melancholy in Niendorf. Linden
has been as overwhelmed, since the news of
the death came last evening, as if his dearest
friend had gone down into the grave with that
limb of Satan. Heaven knows he could not
have been more anxious about a near rela-
tion, and his horses have nearly run their legs
off with making inquiries about the fellow's
health. I really believe he would have given
the doctor of this distinguished citizen a
premium for preserving his precious life."

Uncle Henry grumbled something which
sounded almost like a curse. " Where is
Linden ? " he inquired.

"Upstairs!" replied Miss Adelaide. "He
has been there ever since this morning, at
least we—" indicating the judge and herself
—"dined alone with auntie, then we went to
'Waldruhe' but we did not get in, and now
it is out of sheer desperation that we made a
bowl of *mai-trank*. But won't you taste a
little of it, Mr. Baumhagen?"

She had filled a glass and offered it to the
old gentleman with laughing eyes.

Uncle Henry cast a half-angry, half-eager
glance at the glass in the small hand.

"Witch!" he growled, and marched out of
the room as haughtily as a Spaniard. He was
in too serious a mood to enter into their
"chatter." But a clear laugh sounded behind him.

"I wish the judge would pack that little
monkey in his trunk and send her off to
Frankfort or to Guinea for all I care."

He found the young master of the house at
his writing-table. "Linden," he began, without sitting down, "the carriage is waiting
down-stairs, come with me to your little
wife; if you will only beg her forgiveness,
everything will be all right again."

Frank Linden looked at him calmly.

"Do you know what I should be doing?" he asked—"I should acknowledge a wrong of which I have never been guilty."

"Ah, nonsense! Never mind that! This is the question now, will you have your wife back again or not?"

"Is that the condition on which my wife will return to me?"

"Why, of course. Oh, ta, ta! I am sure at least that she would come then."

"I am sorry, but I cannot do it," replied the young man, growing a shade paler. "It is not for me to beg pardon."

"You are an obstinate set, and that is all there is about it," thundered Uncle Henry. "We are glad that the scoundrel is dead, and now here we are in just the same place as we were before."

"The scoundrel's death is a very unfortunate event for me, uncle."

"You will not?" asked the old gentleman again.

"Ask her pardon—no!"

"Then good-bye!" And Uncle Henry put

on his hat and hastily left the room and the house.

"Allow me to accompany you down," said Frank, following the little man, who jumped into the carriage as if he were fleeing from some one.

But before the horses started he bent forward and an expression of intense anxiety rested on his honest old face.

"See here, Frank," he whispered, "it is a foolish pride of yours. Women have their little whims and caprices. It is true I never had a wife—thank Heaven for that!—but I know them very well for all that. They have such ideas, they must all be worshipped, and the little one is particularly sharp about it. She is like her father, my good old Lebrecht, a little romantic—I always said the child read too much. Now do you be the wise one to give in. You have not been so hurt either, and—besides she is a charming little woman."

"As soon as Gertrude comes back everything shall be forgotten," replied Linden, shutting the carriage door.

"But she won't come so, my boy. Don't

you know the Baumhagen obstinacy yet?"
cried Uncle Henry in despair.

He shrugged his shoulders and stepped
back.

"To Waldruhe!" shouted the old man angrily to the coachman, and away he went.

"My young gentleman is playing a dangerous game as injured innocence," he growled,
pounding his cane on the bottom of the carriage. The nearer he came to the villa, the
redder grew his angry round face. When he
reached "Waldruhe" he did not have to go
upstairs. Gertrude was in the park. She
was standing at the end of a shady alley and
perceiving her uncle she came towards him,
in her simple white summer dress.

"Uncle," she gasped out, and two anxious
eyes sought to read his face.

"Come," said the old man, taking her hand,
"let us walk along this path. It will do me
good. I shall have a stroke if I stand still.
To make my story short, child—he will
not."

"Uncle, what have you done?" cried Gertrude, a flush of mortification covering her
face. "You have been to him?"

" ' Yes,' I said, 'go and ask her forgiveness and everything will come right—women are like that !' and he—"

She pressed her hand on her heart.

" Uncle ! " she cried.

" And he said : No! That would be own-ing a fault which he had not committed. There, my child ! I have tried once more to play the part of peace-maker, but—now I wash my hands of it all. You must do it for yourselves now. Anger is bad for me, as you know, and I have had enough now to last me a month. Good-bye, Gertrude !"

" Good-bye, uncle, I thank you."

He had gone a few steps when the old egotist looked round once more. She was leaning against the trunk of a beech-tree like one who has received a blow. Her eyes were cast down, a strange smile played about her mouth.

" Poor child ! " he stammered out, taking his hat from his burning forehead, and then he went back to her.

" Come now, you must keep your spirits up," he said kindly. " Over there in Nien-dorf that black little monkey was making a *mai-trank* for the judge who is going away. What do you say, Gertrude, shall we go and have some? Come, I will take you over quite quietly. You see we would go so softly into the dining-room, and I am not an egotist if you are not—one—two—three—in each others' arms — you will cry 'Frank!' he will say 'Gertrude!' and all will be forgotten. Gertrude, my good little Gertrude, do be reasonable. Is life so very blissful that one dares fling away the golden days of youth and happiness? Come, come, take my advice just this once."

He had grasped her slender wrist, but she freed herself hastily and her face grew rigid. "No, no, that is all over!" she said in a hard distinct tone.

CHAPTER XIX.

THE summer had come ; the yellowing grain waved in the soft breezes, and the cherry-trees in the orchards and along the high roads had all been robbed of their fruit. The sky was cloudless and the first grain had been harvested in Niendorf.

From the cities every one had fled to the watering-places or into the mountains. The corner-house in the market-place was shut up from top to bottom. Mrs. Baumhagen was in Switzerland, Mr. and Mrs. Fredericks in Baden-Baden. Uncle Henry had gone to Heligoland, because nowhere can one get such good breakfasts as on the dunes of that rocky island.

Only the two sat still in their nests ; separated by a small extent of wood and meadow, they could not have been further apart if the ocean had rolled between. There was no crossing the gulf between them.

In Niendorf everything was irregular and in disorder. How should the little Adelaide know anything about the management of a farm? She was on her feet all day, she took a hundred unnecessary steps, and in the evening she complained that the two dainty little feet in the pointed high-heeled shoes hurt her so, and that the servants had no respect for her. Aunt Rosa was in a bad temper, for she found herself in her old age condemned to the life of a lady-in-waiting. Adelaide could not possibly dine alone with Linden, and she must always be there. So at twelve o'clock every day, the old lady put on her best cap, and sat, the picture of misery, opposite Linden, in Gertrude's vacant place. The meals were desperately melancholy. After awhile Adelaide also became silent, since she very rarely got any reply to her remarks. So they ate their dinner in silence and separated as soon as possible afterwards.

Frank, however, had work to do at least, he could not *always* think and brood and look at the locked door which led into Gertrude's room. That happened in the evening

in his quiet room when little Adelaide was singing all manner of melancholy songs about love and longing down-stairs. And at midnight when it was quite quiet, when every one was asleep in the house and only some faint barking of a dog sounded from the village, he wandered up and down the room till the lamp grew dim and went out, and even then he did not stop.

He no longer expected her to come, though he had done so for days and weeks. At first he had gone to the very walls of her garden with a gnawing desire to see her; he would be there when she came out of the gate, and he would go to meet her at the very first step. In vain, she did not come.

Once the servants had seen him when his eyes were strangely red. "The master is crying for the mistress," was the report in the kitchen.

"Why doesn't he go and get her?" said the coachman, "I wouldn't cry a drop; I should know very well how to get back an obstinate wife," making an unmistakable gesture. "Brute!" cried the maids, and thereupon all the women turned their backs on him.

It was long since there had been such a harvest; the barns could scarcely contain all the grain. The fragrance of the hay came over from the meadows and mingled with that of the thousand roses in the garden; the great linden bloomed in the court-yard and a happy hen-mother led out to walk a legion of yellow little chickens.

In the stork's nest on the barn the young ones were growing apace; the homely old house lay almost buried in luxuriant greenery; the clematis climbed up to the windows and peeped in at the empty rooms, and the swallows which were building under the roof, went crying through the country and the city, "She has gone away from him! She has gone away from him!"

Yes, everybody knew the sad story by this time. Gertrude Baumhagen was separated from her husband. In the coffee parties one whispered to the other, people spoke of it at the cafés and at dinner-parties, and at the table d'hôte in the hotel it was the standing topic of conversation. No one knew exactly why this had happened. There were a thousand reports of a most wonderful nature.

" He did something disagreeable about his wife's dowry—"

" She went away because he lifted his hand to strike her—"

" The mother-in-law made mischief between them—"

" Nonsense ! She was jealous—there is a little brown cousin in the house—"

" No, it was not that—she heard that before they were engaged he consulted an agent about her fortune. It is not so very unusual now-a-days."

" Ah, bah, no woman would run away for that ! "

" That shows that you don't know Gertrude Baumhagen very well. It is a fact that she has gone away."

Yes, it was a fact, and Gertrude sat in her lonely house like one buried alive in that ever gloomy room. She could no longer read ; it seemed as if she slept with open eyes. Sometimes Johanna brought her her child, and the young wife's eyes mechanically followed the little creature as it crept awkwardly over the floor or tried to raise itself by a chair, but she would not touch it even when it fell and cried.

—Towards evening, however, the same un-accountable restlessness always came over her ; then she walked hurriedly up and down the garden for a long time till she reached the top of the little hill; there she would remain for hours, gazing at the Thurmberg till her hair and dress were wet with dew.

" Believe me," she said to Johanna, " I shall be ill—here," and she pointed to her head."

" I do believe it," assented the other, " it is easy to make one's self ill—"

It was a day at the end of July; a frightful sultry heat brooded over the earth, and the young wife suffered greatly from it even in her cool room. After dinner she lay motion-less in her chair by the window; a severe headache tortured her as was so often the case lately.

Johanna placed her cupful of strong black coffee on the table and put the book beside it which had been opened at the same page for the last three days.

" Here is a letter too," she added.

Gertrude had acquired a great dread of letters lately. She overcame her aversion however and opened it. It was in Jenny's pointed handwriting, and Jenny only wrote surface gossip; one glance at the letter would suffice. Two sheets fell out.

"It is a long time since we heard anything from you," she read, "so that we are very anxious about you—are you still in 'Wald-ruhe?'"

"I met Judge K. yesterday at a reception, the same who, in the celebrated divorce case of the Duke of P. with Countess Y., was the counsel of the latter. I asked him playfully if a woman could separate from her lord and master if she found that he had had more thought of her worldly goods than of herself, described the situation pretty plainly and spoke of a friend of mine who was in such a position. He replied, 'Tell your friend she had better go quietly back to her husband, for she is sure to get the worst of it.' His real expression was a much rougher one, for he is well known as a brute.

"Well, there you have the opinion of an authority in such matters. Make an end of the matter, for you may have so bitterly to re-pent a longer delay as you are quite unable to realize in your present magnificent scorn. If

I am not much mistaken you really love him. Well, there are things—but it is hard to write about such things. Read the enclosed letter, which mamma sent me a few days ago. Perhaps you will guess what I wanted to say.

" I wish you had been with me in Paris or were here now in Baden-Baden. You would see how we German women, with our thick-skinned housewifely virtues and our cobwebby romance, make our lives unnecessarily hard. I am convinced a French woman would hold her sides for laughing if she should hear the cause of your conjugal strife.

"Arthur is very amiable, and obeys at a word. He surprised me with a Paris dress for the reception yesterday. As soon as he gets out of our little nest he is like another man. Good-bye, don't take this affair too tragically.

"Your Sister."

Slowly the young wife took up the other letter; it was in Aunt Pauline's pointed hand-writing and was addressed to Mrs. Baum-hagen.

" DEAREST OTTILIE :

" Everything here goes on as usual. I was at your house yesterday ; Sophie is there and had a great moth-hunt yesterday. Your parrot had a bad eye but it is all right again now. I have heard nothing of Gertrude ; she will let nobody in. I suppose you have heard from her. There are all sorts of reports about Niendorf going about. Last evening my husband came home from the club—they say there is a cousin there who manages the house. Mr. Hanke has seen her in Linden's carriage—very dark, rather original, and very much dressed. Well, of course, you know how people will talk, but I will not pour oil on the fire. I saw Linden too, once, and I hardly knew him ; he was coming from the bank. The man's hair is growing gray about the temples ; he looked like another person, so—how shall I describe it—so run down."

Gertrude dropped the letter and then she sprang up—she shook and trembled in every limb.

With a powerful effort she forced herself to be calm and to be reasonable. What did she wish ? She had separated from him forever. But her heart ! her heart hurt her so all at once, and it beat so loudly in the deathly

18

stillness which surrounded her that she thought she could hear it.

"Johanna!" she shrieked, but no one replied; she was probably out in the garden or in the kitchen at work.

And what good could she do her? "No, not that, only not that!"

She sat down again in her chair by the window and looked out among the trees. What would she not give if the woods and the hills would disappear so that she could look across into that house—into that room! "A gay little thing is that brown little girl," Johanna had said the other day. And Gertrude saw her in her mind's eye tripping about the house, now in the garden-hall, now up the steps, those dear old worn-out steps. Tap, tap, now in the corridor, the high-heeled shoes tapped so firmly and daintily on the hard floor; and now at a brown door—his door.

Might she enter? Ah, his room, that dear old room! And Gertrude wrung her hands in bitter envy. "Go!" she cried, half-aloud, "go! That threshold is sacred—I—I crossed it on the happiest day of my life—on his arm!"

And she could see him sitting at his writing-table in his gray jacket and his high boots
just as he had come in from the fields; his
white forehead stood out in sharp contrast to
his brown face.   She had always liked that.

And gray hair on his temples?   Ah, he had
none a few weeks ago!

And again a dainty little figure fluttered
before her eyes going towards him.   Ah, she
would like to know that one thing—if he could
ever forget her for another—for this girl perhaps?   But of what use was all this?

She got up and went out of the room across
the corridor to her father's room.   What her
father had done thousands had done before
him, and thousands would do it—a man need
not live!

On the table by the bed stood the glass with
his monogram, out of which he had drunk
that dreadful potion.   The servants had
washed it and put it back there.   She walked
a few steps toward the window and started
suddenly.   Ah yes, it was only her image in
the glass.   She walked quickly up to the
shining glass and looked in—there was a wonderful bluish shimmer in it and her face, pale

•

as death, looked out at her from it. The deep shadows under the eyes spread far down on her cheeks. Shuddering, she turned away; there was something ghostly about her own face.

And again she stood still and thought. What was left for her in life? Everything was gone with him, everything!

"Mrs. Linden," said a voice behind her, "Judge Schmidt."

She nodded.

"In my room."

Ah, yes, she had forgotten that she had sent for him. He came to-day, and she had only written yesterday. But it was just as well, she must make a beginning.

She turned back again; let him wait, she could not go just yet. She went to the window and saw how the heavy leaden clouds were spreading over the sky; a storm was brewing in the west. Courage, now, courage! When it was past the sun would shine again; sometimes a broken branch could not lift itself again. So much the better! There would be no more of this quiet, this deadly calm.

Only something to do—even if—

" Ma'am ! " called the voice once more, and then she composed herself and went.

She knew him very well, the old gentleman who came towards her with a kind smile, but she could not speak a word to him. She could only wave her hand silently towards the nearest chair. He knew what the matter was, let him begin the dreadful conversation.

" You wish for my advice, Mrs. Linden, in this difficult matter ? "

" Yes, I wish you to act for me," she said, looking past him into the corner of the room, " and I wish above all that Mr. Linden should be informed of the decision I have come to. I will leave him in possession of my whole fortune with the exception of this house, and the capital that is invested in my brother-in-law's factory."

She said the words hurriedly, as if she had learned them by heart.

" Are you quite in earnest about it then ? " asked the old man.

Her eyes blazed out at him.

" Do you think I would jest on such a sorrowful subject ? "

" And you think your husband will agree ? "

" It is *your* affair, Mr. Schmidt, to arrange this."

He bowed without speaking. She too was silent. An oppressive stillness reigned in the room, in the whole house. It seemed to Gertrude as if she had just heard her sentence of death.

" There will be a bad storm to-day," said the judge after awhile. " I must leave you now, madam, and as I am half-way to Niendorf now, I will just drive over, to arrange the matter with your husband in person."

" To-day ? " She was startled into saying it.

He hesitated and looked at her.

" You are right, to-morrow will suit me better too—let us say the day after to-morrow."

" No," she replied, hastily, " go at once, it will be better, much better."

She got up in some confusion ; her headache, the consciousness that she had now set the ball rolling nearly overwhelmed her. She accompanied the lawyer mechanically to the head of the stairs ; then she remained standing in the corridor, her hand pressing her throbbing temples, half unconscious.

She could hear Johanna in the kitchen, and as if she could bear the loneliness no longer she went in and sat down on a chair beside the white scoured table. Johanna was standing before it, choosing between ivy-leaves and cypress-twigs. Her eyes were red with crying, and large drops fell now and then on the hands which were making a wreath. The whole kitchen smelled of death and funerals.

"What are you doing there?" asked Gertrude.

Johanna looked away and suppressed a sob.

"It will be a year to-morrow," she replied in a choked voice, "since they brought him home to me dead."

"Ah, true."

The two women looked deep into each other's sorrowful eyes, each with the thought that she was the most unhappy. Ah, but there stood the little carriage with the sleeping child, and that belonged to Johanna, and Johanna could think of *him* without other sorrow and heartache than that for his loss. To lose a loved one by death, is not half so hard as to lose him in life. Gertrude could find no word of sympathy.

"Oh, how could I live through it!" sobbed the young widow. "So fresh and strong as he went across the threshold, I think I can see him now striding up the street. And the very night before, we had a little quarrel for the first time and I thought, 'Just you wait, you will have to beg for a pleasant word from me.' And I went to bed without saying good night, and the next morning I wouldn't make his coffee.

"I heard him moving about in the room and I was glad to think that he would have to go without his breakfast. He came to my bed once and looked in my face and I pretended to be asleep. But as soon as he had shut the outside door behind him, I jumped up and ran to the window and looked after him—I was so proud of him. It was the last time; it wasn't two hours later when they brought him home, and day and night I was on my knees before him, shrieking, and asking if he was angry with me still. And I prayed to God that He would let him open his eyes just once, only once, so I could say, 'Good-bye, Fritz, come home safe, Fritz.' But it was all of no use; he never heard me any more."

Gertrude sprang up suddenly and left the kitchen. O God! She felt sick unto death. Everything seemed to whirl round and round in her brain, as if her mind were unsettled. She could no longer follow out a train of thought to its end, and an idea which had seized upon her five minutes ago in the most horrible clearness, she was now unable to recall; try as hard as she might, nothing remained to her but a dull dread of something dreadful hanging over her.

It was no doubt the heavy air, the oppressive stillness of nature before a storm that had so excited her nerves.

She rang for ice-water. When Johanna set the glass before her she turned her head away.

"Johanna, do you happen to know how long the—young lady is going to stay at Niendorf?"

"I think the whole summer, ma'am," was the reply. "A good thing, too. What could they do without her over there?"

Gertrude bit her lip; she felt ashamed. What right had *she* to ask about it?

"Did you want anything more, ma'am?"

" Nothing, thanks."

And she remained alone in her room as she had been so many days before. She could hear the gnawing of the moths in the old wood-work, and now and then the steps of the servant in the corridor. With burning eyes she gazed at the ever-darkening sky; her hands grasped the slender arm of her chair as if they must have an outward support at least.

Gradually it began to grow dark; the approaching evening and the black storm-clouds together soon made it quite dusk, while now and then sharp flashes of lightning brought the dark trees into full relief. Close by Johanna was closing the windows of the sleeping-room.

" Shall I bring a lamp?" she asked, looking through the half-opened door.

" No, thanks."

" But you oughtn't to sit so near the window, ma'am, it looks so dreadful out there."

Gertrude did not move and the tear-stained face disappeared. A sudden gust of wind swept through the trees, the branches were tossed wildly about as if in a fierce struggle with brute force; the slender branches were bent down to the ground only to rise again as quickly, and a fierce blast whirling about gravel, leaves and small stones dashed them against the rattling panes. Then followed a dazzling flash of lightning, thunder that made the house shake, and at the same time a sudden deluge of rain mingled with the peculiar pattering of large hail-stones.

Johanna, with her child in her arms, came anxiously into her mistress' room.

"Oh, mercy!" she shrieked, falling on her knees before the nearest chair. Another flash filled the room for a moment with a dazzling red light, and the thunder crashed after it like a thousand cannon.

"That struck, Mrs. Linden, that struck!" cried she in terror.

Gertrude had stepped back from the window; she was standing in the middle of the room. By the light of the constant flashes the servant could see her pale, rigid face with perfect distinctness. She rested her hands on the table and looked towards the window as if it did not concern her in the least. And still the storm raged more fiercely, while the world seemed to be standing in a perfect sea of fire. It seemed to have endured for hours. But gradually the flashes grew less frequent, the crashes of thunder grew more distant, and at last only a light rain dripped on the trees and the storm died away in a distant low grumbling.

Gertrude opened the window and bent far out; a wonderfully sweet air blew upon her face, soft and aromatic, refreshing and invigorating, and above in the sky the clouds had parted and a brilliant star sparkled down upon her. Then she started back. From the high-road there came a sound of hurried movements; a sound of wheels, the cracking of whips, the cries of men—what did it mean? It was usually as quiet as the grave here at this hour.

" Fire ! " Had she heard aright? She could not see the street but she leaned far out and listened to the uproar. Her heart beat loud and fast. The gardener's wife ran hastily up in her clattering wooden shoes, and her shrill voice came up to Gertrude's ears.

" David, hurry, hurry, hurry, it has been

burning in Niendorf for the last half-hour—
the engine has just gone by—hurry!"

"Clang, clang, clang!" clashed out the
church bell now. In Gertrude's ears it
sounded like a death-knell. Clang, clang,
clang! Why did she stand still there, her
hands clasping the window-sill as if they were
nailed there? She heard doors banging, and
voices and shouts, she heard the gardener
rushing out of his house—and still she stood
there as if there was a spell upon her.

Again clashed out the warning notes of the
bell! And at length she roused herself as if
from a heavy dream, and now she was quite
alive once more. She flew like an arrow out
of the room, snatched a shawl from the wall
of the corridor and rushed past Johanna, who
was standing at the gate with the gardener's
wife and children,—away out over the half-
flooded high-road.

"Mrs. Linden! For the love of Heaven!"
screamed Johanna behind her. But she paid
no heed to the cry. Like a murmured prayer
came from her lips—"On! on!"

The road before her was dark and lonely;

the men who had hastened to the rescue, were out of sight long ago.

She actually flew ; she felt no fear in the gloomy wood ; she saw nothing but the dear old burning house, and a pair of manly eyes— once, ah, once so inexpressibly dear. Something came pattering behind her. Ah, yes— the dog.

"Come," she murmured, and hurried on, the sagacious animal close behind her.

CHAPTER XX.

It was a long way to Niendorf, but Gertrude flew as if she had wings.

"Good Heavens!" she groaned as she reached the top of the hill and saw the red glow in the sky. Faster and faster she rushed down the hill; at the next turn she must see Niendorf—and at last she stood there, breathing quick and loud, her eyes gazing with terror into the valley. Thank God! The red smoke was still rising into the sky, the flames still shot up here and there, but the force of the fire was broken. It is true, shouts and cries still sounded in her ears, but already she met men who were going home.

She moved aside into the deepest shadow and gazed down into the valley; the old house stood there safe and sound, the red light of the dying flames played about its green ivy-wreathed gables and lighted up the shrubs in the garden. The barns were in

ruins to be sure, but what mattered that? As
she stood there gazing at the house with insa-
tiable eyes, a light suddenly shone out behind
two of the windows, gazing at her like a pair
of friendly eyes. The windows were his.
But the young wife found nothing reassuring
in them. The terrible anxiety which had left
her at the sight of the uninjured house, suddenly leaped up with renewed force. How
happened it that there should be lights in his
room when the fire was still smouldering
down there? He in the house when his
presence below was so necessary?

No, never—or he must—

On—on—only to see—only to see from a
distance, whether he lived and was well!

"Life hangs on the merest thread," Johanna's words sounded in her ears. "God in
Heaven, have mercy, do not punish me *so!*"

At the garden-gate she stopped. What
should she do here? Her ambassador had
come here only to-day and had offered him
money for her freedom. Ah, freedom!

Of what use is it when the heart is still
held fast in chains and bands? And she ran
in under the dark trees of the garden, round

the little pond, on the surface of which a faint
rosy shimmer of the dying fire still played,
and she sank exhausted on a garden-chair
under the chestnuts ; just in front of her, only
across the gravel walk was the house and a
dim light shone out of the garden-hall.

Upstairs, the bright light was gone from
his windows; shouts and voices of men still
came up from the court, carriages were being
pulled about, horses taken out, all mingled
with the sharp hissing sound of the hose.
Gertrude shivered ; a great weakness had
come over her, her temples throbbed, the
smell of the fire nearly took her breath
away.

Here she sat motionless, gazing at the steps
which led to the garden-hall. Her eyes
sought out step after step and at last lingered
in the door. "Up there! In there!" she
thought, her heart beating wildly, but pride
and shame held her fast as with iron chains.

It gradually grew quieter in the court, then
steps approached, firm, elastic steps. Gertrude quickly seized the dog by the collar.
"Down, Diana!" she cried, hoarse with terror, and then a figure passed the bright light

19

of the window, and brushing close by her went into the house.

Frank! He was alive—thank God! But he was hurt, he kept his arm pressed so closely to his side. Ah, but he was alive! and now, now she could go again quietly and unperceived as she had come. There were plenty of hands in there to bind up his wounds, to—

She shivered again as if in fever.

"Come," she said to the whining dog, and she got up and turned away towards the darker paths, but the dog pressed eagerly toward the house, and almost as if she knew not what she was doing she suffered herself to be dragged forward by him.

At length she reached the steps and in another moment she was mounting them. Only one look inside, only to see if he really was suffering, if he really was alive! And holding the impatient animal still more firmly she passed noiselessly across the stone terrace; then she leaned against the door-post and peeped through the glass, trembling with emotion, timorous as a thief, full of longing as a child on Christmas Eve.

The room looked just as usual, the carpets, the pictures, all just as she had left it ; within were people hurrying busily to and fro, and by the table near the lamp he was sitting, his face, pale and drawn with pain, turned full towards the door. And beside him, bending over him, and binding up his arm with all the charming grace of an anxious and tender wife, was the agile little creature in a black dress and white apron, her bunch of keys stuck in her girdle. How skilfully she laid on the bandage ! With what supple, tapering fingers she fastened it ! How nearly her dark hair touched his face !

And this must be done by other hands than these that she was wringing so here outside !

A joyful bark sounded beside her, and the dog broke away from her trembling fingers with a sudden spring and bounded against the door so that it shook. She started to flee in terror, but her strength failed her ; the ground seemed to sway under her feet, half-unconscious she could still hear the door hastily torn open, and then she lost consciousness altogether.

CHAPTER XXI.

GERTRUDE awoke, just as the day began to dawn, from a deep dreamless sleep. She was not ill, and she knew perfectly well what had happened to her the evening before. She was lying on the sofa in Aunt Rosa's room; above her smiled down the ancestress with the powdered hair, and the whole wonderful rose-wreathed room was in the full glow of the morning sunshine.

At the foot of the bed on a low footstool sat a young girl in a black dress and a white apron; the dark head had fallen against the arm of the sofa—Adelaide was sound asleep.

The young wife got up softly. Her drenched clothing had been taken off the night before and her own dressing-gown put on; there was still a large part of her wardrobe in Niendorf; she even found her dainty slippers standing before the sofa, which she was accustomed to put on when she got up.

She was very quick and very careful not to wake the young girl. But as she softly opened the door, the sleeper sprang up, and a pair of wondering dark eyes gazed up at Gertrude.

"Where are you going?" asked the clear voice.

Gertrude stopped, undecided.

" Mr. Linden went to bed so very late," continued Adelaide Strom ; "he sat here beside you till about an hour ago. You will not wake him ? It is not four o'clock yet."

A pair of firm little hands drew the young wife away from the door towards the sofa, and in contradiction to the childish words a pair of grave eyes looked at her, saying plainly, " Do what you will—I shall not let you go."

Gertrude sat down again on the improvised bed and bit her lips till they bled, but the young girl busied herself at a side-table, and presently a fragrant odor of coffee filled the room.

"Here," she said, offering the young wife a cup of the hot beverage, " take it, it will do you good. I made some coffee for Mr. Linden too, in the night: only drink it quietly, it

is *his* cup and no one else has ever touched
it."

And as Gertrude made no reply and only
held the cup in her trembling hand without
drinking, Adelaide continued without taking
any notice—

"Ah, yesterday was a dreadful day. The
frightful storm and that dreadful thunderbolt,
and the great barn was in flames in a
moment, and before any help came the other
was burning, and it was with the greatest
difficulty the animals were saved. If Mr.
Linden had not been so calm and had so
much presence of mind, it would have been
frightful. But he went into the horses' stable
just as if the flames were not darting in after
him, and he put the harness on the horses
and they followed him out through the flames
like lambs, though no one could get them out
before. And only think, when the uproar
was the greatest, and the fire was sending
showers of sparks into the air, as if they were
rockets, something began to howl and cry
so loud from the very top of the barn, and we
found it was Lora, the great St. Bernard dog,
who had puppies up there.

" And how that poor dumb creature did cry
out for help! I could hear from my window
that no one would go up after her,—" Being a
dog," they all said. And all at once I saw a
ladder, and one—two—three—a figure disappeared up there in the flames. What do you
think, Mr. Linden brought them all down, the
old dog and her young ones—all of them."

The little girl's eyes sparkled with tears.

" But he has a mark of it on his arm to be
sure," she added, "and it was only a dog
after all. What was it in comparison with a
man's life?—Aunt Rosa was so angry with
him and said, when he came down here pale
and suffering with the pain, he might have
lost his life. Then he said that such a stupid
thing as his life wasn't worth a straw! And
just as he had said it, Diana began to scratch
so furiously at the door, and he rushed out at
such a rate that I thought the lightning must
have struck again, and as I ran out behind
him, he had you already in his well arm, and
declared that he knew you would come."

Gertrude got up at this point, and walked
to the door. But here she met another ob-
stacle. This was Aunt Rosa, who was just

coming out of her bedroom in the most astonishing morning array and the most enormous
white nightcap that a lady ever wore. She
nodded to Gertrude, and laid her small withered hand on her shoulder.

"The dear God always opens a way for the
hard heart to soften," said the ancient dame.
"Yes, in hour of need, the heart has wings
on which it is lifted above all the petty foolish-
ness of pride and perversity. It was just before the closing of the door, too, my dear
child, for yesterday afternoon, after a certain
man had had an interview with him, I folded
my hands and prayed to God to give him
strength to bear the blow—I was afraid he
would never get over it."

Adelaide Strom now went softly out of the
door and the old woman remained standing
before the young wife, and the tall form
seemed almost to shrink beneath her thin
transparent hand. But neither spoke. The
eastern sky grew redder, and then the first rays
of the sun played on Gertrude's brown hair.

Suddenly she covered her face with her
hands. "My happiness is over, I can never be
anything more to him!" she gasped.

"Say rather ' I *will* never be anything more to him !' "

"Ah, and even if I would!" she cried, " I am so wretched!"

" He who will not do a thing willingly and gladly would do better to leave it undone, and he who cares not to pray, should not fold his hands." And Aunt Rosa turned away to the window, sat down in her easy chair and took up her prayer-book. She left Gertrude to herself and read her morning chapter half aloud.

The words struck the ear of the struggling girl with a wonderful force.

" 'Though I speak with the tongues of men and of angels and have not charity—" sounded through the room.

"Charity suffereth long and is kind ; beareth all things, believeth all things, hopeth all things, endureth all things."

Had she no charity then, no true love? Ah, faith—love—how should they remain when one has been so cruelly deceived ! And her house came back to her mind, that sad, lonely house on the edge of the wood, and her life in the last few weeks, so frightfully bare and desolate.

And—"charity beareth all things—" it said.

"Amen!" said Aunt Rosa, aloud. And Adelaide came in, and the young wife suddenly felt her hands drawn down and through her tears she saw Adelaide, smilingly unlocking the bunch of keys from her own belt and holding it out to her.

"I kept things in order as well as I knew how," she said, "it is not in the most perfect order I know, but you must not scold me."

She felt the keys put into her nerveless hand—had she not been bowed down into the dust?

"Charity suffereth long and is kind; charity vaunteth not itself," said something in her heart.

"I will forgive him," said the young wife aloud. But her face was pale and rigid.

"Forgive, with *those* eyes?" asked Aunt Rosa. "And for what? For believing him less than an acknowledged—well, he is dead, God forgive him—than a man who was a perfect stranger to you? No, my little woman, take heart and go up to your Frank and—"

"*I* go to *him?*" she cried in cutting tones, —"*I?*" The bunch of keys fell clanging on the floor ; with trembling hands she snatched up the dress she had worn the day before, and took the purse out of the pocket,—the purse which contained that fatal scrap of paper. For awhile she held the piece of paper in her hand, then she gave it to the old lady.

"I will not seem to you so childishly perverse," she said.

Aunt Rosa put on her glasses and read it. She started, and then a smile spread over her face. In great confusion she looked into Gertrude's face.

"Addie," she said, "you can bear witness that I have always been a most orderly person my whole life long."

"Yes, auntie, the most envious person must allow you that virtue."

"And yet last Christmas it happened to me to mislay a letter. It was to Linden from Wolff ; for four whole days we searched for it. Let me see, that was the twenty-second of December—the letter was lost, and on the twenty-sixth, I happened to lift up my window-cushion and there was the thing. No one could have been gladder than I. I stayed up till late at night—Linden had gone to

a party at the Baumhagens—and when at last
he came home I gave him the letter and he
put it carelessly in his pocket and said,
'Aunt Rosa, you shall hear it first, I have
just been getting engaged.' And in the joy
of his heart he took me in his arms as if I
were still only eighteen. You see, and that "
—she struck the bit of paper with her right
hand—"that is a scrap of the letter, my little
woman, and the date coincides exactly."

Gertrude was already by her side. "Is
that true?" escaped from her trembling lips.

The old lady nodded. "Perfectly true,"
she declared. "Ask Dora. She searched
for the letter with me, and thereby got a great
knock on the head when she was trying to
move the wardrobe."

But Gertrude declined this. She stood for
awhile in silence, her head bent down, her
color changing rapidly from red to white, then
she moved towards the door and in another
moment she had disappeared.

Lightly she mounted the stairs, and the old
worn boards seemed to understand why the
little feet stepped so carefully and did not as
usual, crack and snap.

It was still as death in the whole house; the corridor was still dusky and the old pictures on the wall looked sleepily down on the young wife. The tall clock kept on its solemn tick-tack, tick-tack. It sounded so strangely in Gertrude's ears, as she stood hesitating before the brown door and grasped the knob.

Tick-tack, tick-tack! How the time flies! One should not hesitate a moment when one has a fault to repair—every minute is so much taken from him—quick, quick!

Softly she opened the door and slipped in. She had drawn her dress close about her, so the train should not rustle. Two large eyes gazed anxiously out of the pale face round the room, which was glowing in the morning sunshine. Now her heart seemed to stop beating for a moment, now it throbbed wildly: there in the large chair—he had not gone to bed, but sleep had overtaken him. There he sat, his wounded arm rested on the arm of the chair, the other supported his head. He wore still the soiled, singed coat he had on the day before, and ah, he looked so pale, so changed!

The dog, which lay at his feet, lifted up his

head and wagged his tail. Then she went towards him. "Make way for me," she murmured, "*I* must take that place!"

And she knelt down before her husband, and taking the shrinking injured hand put it to her lips.

"Gertrude, what are you doing?"

"Forgive me, Frank, forgive me?" she whispered, weeping, resisting his endeavors to raise her.

"No, Frank, no, let me stay here, it should be so—"

"Forgive you? There is no question of that. Thank God you are here again!"

But before she got up she tore a bit of paper into shreds, then she ran to the window and opened her hand and they danced away in the air like snowflakes. And when she turned back again she looked into his grave eyes.

"What was that?" he asked, drawing her towards him.

She threw her arms round his neck and hid her streaming eyes on his breast. They stood thus together at the open window, in the clear rays of the morning sun. The twittering swallows flew past them over the tops of the trees up into the blue sky.

"Back again! Back again!" was the burden of their song.

Gradually the house woke up. The little brunette laid the table in the garden-hall.

"Two cups, two plates, and a bunch of roses in the middle—for the last time," said she, "then she can do it for herself again."

Then she stood thinking for a moment.

"He doesn't in the least realize how fortunate he is to get such a yielding, lamb-like wife as I am," she murmured. "To be sure, I *could* not possibly fancy that he married me for my money."

She laughed a clear ringing laugh.

"I shall have a nice little trousseau if Aunt Rosa gets it."

And she opened the garden door and ran out into the green shrubbery.

The world was so beautiful, the sun so golden and Adelaide was so fond of the little judge.

She was engaged, secretly engaged, for the good fellow would not come before his friend in all his bridegroom's bliss, when his happiness was so utterly shattered. So they had plighted their troth secretly—after the bowl of *mai-trank* on that last day. Aunt Rosa was no check upon them, for she slept placidly in the corner of the sofa, and Frank—Heaven alone knew when he had gone.

But now—she looked at her pretty little hands; yes, there were ink-stains on them; she had sent off the news at once to Frankfort : "Great fire, great anxiety, great reconciliation."

She found herself suddenly before a stout little man in a gray summer overcoat and a white straw hat.

"Oh, ta, ta! little one, don't run over me!"

He was very cross, this good Uncle Henry.

"Pretty state of affairs! A man comes from Hamburg, travelling all night, and hardly is he out of the train when some one comes : "Mr. Baumhagen, did you know there had been a great fire in Niendorf?" Tired as a dog as I was, I must needs get into a carriage and drive out here—a man can't sleep after such a piece of news as that. For mercy's sake, you are smiling as if it was Christmas eve!"

"All the crops are burnt," announced Adelaide in as joyful a tone as if she had said, "We have won a great prize."

"The poor fellow has ill-luck," muttered Uncle Henry. "Has some one gone over to —" He would not speak her name—"to—well, to ' Waldruhe ?' Or has the announcement of the joyful news been left for me again ?"

"No one has been there," replied Adelaide, mischievously.

Uncle Henry looked at her more sharply.

"Well, what's up then, you witch ? Something has happened."

"I am engaged," burst out the happy little bride. Thank Heaven, that she could tell it at last.

"You unhappy child !" cried Uncle Henry, by way of congratulation. But she ran laughing away into the house.

"Breakfast is ready !" she cried from the terrace. "Coffee, tea, ham and eggs."

The old gentleman, who was going out to view the wreck, turned sharply round and followed her.

"It is true," he remarked, "I shall be bet-

20

ter for having something to eat ; I am quite upset by the journey."

And Uncle Henry went puffing up the steps and grasped the door-knob.

Good Heavens!—did his eyes not deceive him? There sat Linden, his arm in a sling, and beside him—surely he knew that thick brown knot of hair and that slender figure which was bending down to cut up his meat. Now she raises her head and kisses him on the forehead before she quietly resumes her own place.

" Angels and ministers of grace defend us ! A man has only to take a journey—! "

Uncle Henry drops the door-knob. He has such a queer sensation—he does not like emotion—and he does not like to disturb other people. He would gladly get out of the way if he could—perhaps he may manage it yet.

But no. Gertrude herself opens the door.

" Uncle Henry," she said, pleadingly.

And he comes in and behaves exactly as if nothing had ever happened. It is the purest selfishness on his part. Scenes don't agree with him.

" I wanted just to see how you were—you

seem to have had a nice little fire,' he begins.

"Thank God! No lives were lost," said Linden, "and no cattle were burnt; the crops are all destroyed, it is true; but in place of that a new life has risen out of the ashes." And he held out his sound hand to Gertrude.

"Oh, ta, ta!" murmured Uncle Henry, helping himself hurriedly to ham and to butter. "I tell you, children, travelling is a great deal too hard work, and if it were not for the lobsters in Heligoland and the eel-soup in Hamburg, then—but, Gertrude, you are laughing and crying at the same time! Well, well, I am glad to be home again; there is nothing like home, after all, and with your permission, I will drink this glass of good port wine to your health and to the peace and prosperity of your household."

www.ingramcontent.com/pod-product-compliance
Lightning Source LLC
Chambersburg PA
CBHW060515030726
47498CB00004B/952